By Christopher Dow

I0549120

Fiction
Effigy
    Book I: Stroud
    Book II: Oakdale
The Books of Bob
    Devil of a Time
    Jumping Jehovah
The Clay Guthrie Mysteries
    The Dead Detective
    Landscape with Beast
    The Texas Troll Unlimited
    Darkness Insatiable
Roadkill
The Werewolf and Tide, and other Compulsions

Nonfiction
Lord of the Loincloth (nonfiction novel)
The Wellspring: An Inquiry into the Nature of Chi
Circling the Square: Observations on the Dynamics of Tai Chi
    Chuan
Elements of Power: Essays on the Art and Practice of Tai Chi
    Chuan
Alchemy of Breath: An Introduction to Chi Kung
Book of Curiosities: Adventures in the Paranormal
Occasional Pilgrimage: Essays on Film, Literature, and Other Matters
Living the Story: The Meandering, True, and Sometimes Strange
    Adventures of an Unknown Writer
    Vol.I: Growing Up Takes a Long Time
    Vol. II: Growing Old Takes Longer

Poetry
City of Dreams
The Trip Out
Texas White Line Fever
Networks
A Dilapidation of Machinery
Puzzle Pieces: Selected Poems

Editor
The Abby Stone: The Poetry of Bartholo Dias
The Best of Phosphene
The Best of Dialog

THE WEREWOLF AND TIDE

THE WEREWOLF AND TIDE

AND
OTHER COMPULSIONS

CHRISTOPHER DOW

Phosphene Publishing Company
Temple, Texas

The Werewolf and Tide, and Other Compulsions
© 2014 by Christopher Dow
ISBN 13: 978-0-9851477-2-3
ISBN 10: 0985147725

Published by
Phosphene Publishing Company
Temple, Texas, U.S.A.
phosphenepublishing.com

The following stories have appeared previously:

"Meetings with Arthur," Dialog, vI, #1, Feb. 1983.
"Rimbeau's Women," Phosphene, vI, #1, 1978.

2.2

For Ditto
Thanks for your friendship and support.

CONTENTS

THE WEREWOLF AND TIDE

THE WEREWOLF AND TIDE

SHE WAS NEAR. HE KNEW it, though his eyes saw only darkness. Snarling at her salty scent rising in a wave around him, he lashed out in the blackness. A single wisp of hair whirling through the night brushed through his talons. Then the wisp escaped, and her mocking laughter rang in his ears.

Lunging and stumbling through the darkness, he pursued her, sometimes so close he could feel the dank breath of her passage. He was empty of thought, full of dark, raging passion. Gradually her presence melted into the inky distances, and he stopped, panting, trying to orient himself. Suddenly she was beside him, taunting, teasing, calling. Again he pursued her through the night, viciously, futilely. Then he awoke, and she was gone so thoroughly that nothing of her remained but vague unease.

Tangled branches rustled in a slight breeze, fracturing the slanting rays of morning sunlight into splinters over his sprawled form. As his gummy eyes opened, the light whirled his disoriented vision into vertigo. He groaned and pressed the back of a hand against his face. The coarse, grimy, blood-crusted fur grated harshly against his cheek, bringing him back to the reality of his condition. Groaning once more, he tried to sit up, but pain shooting through his lower back drained the strength from him, and he collapsed to his side. Gradually, the cramping subsided, and he opened his eyes.

Earth and leaves half obscured his vision. He tried to straighten himself, then realized he was as straight as he could get. Not human, nor fully beast, he was caught in the numb agony of the between state he had come to despise for its vulnerability. He would lie here all day, unable to move more than a few yards, until dusk and the rising moon restored the power to cast off the enthralling cape of humanity that half draped him.

Only in Luna's opalescent light could he run wild, free, and full of power, exalting in his dominance. He knew this instinctively rather than with true memory, for he could never remember. The dusk that brought the moon and his power also brought a pall of darkness to shroud his recollection of the events of the night.

He rolled painfully onto his stomach and, dragging his almost paralyzed hindquarters, crawled from beneath the hedgerow, over to a nearby tree. Once there, he propped himself against the trunk as best as he could. It was always like this during the days of the full moon. He would wake twisted and half-unformed, malaise permeating him. His hunched body was covered in fur and ragged swaths of clothing.

Thirst rasped in his throat, but the gentle breeze brought no scent of nearby water. Worse, though, was the hunger—an utterly voracious craving for more than food. It came at the onset of the illness and, at night, blossomed in his belly into a ravening that he could never seem to apprehend. Appease it, though, he evidently did, for it was always gone when he regained normalcy, the rank blood splashed and dried on his body mute testimony to the method of its satiation.

He forced down the self disgust that surged from his inability to control his lunacy rather than from such prosaic origins as remorse or guilt. When he first realized the extent of his illness, he had become determined to beat it down and conquer it with the force of his will. He viewed his disease as a challenge to overcome, but that it had arisen at all as a blot on his self-sufficiency.

He knew he was a werewolf, a lycanthrope. How could he fail to know this terrible truth? That fact, most apparent in his physical transformation, lay equally embedded in his every fiber. He had only to sense, just below the surface, the unknown forces that plucked and twisted at the very core of his being; forces that were always there but that, for three days each month, annealed into a raging blackness shot through with burning passion that spun crazily through him, endowed with an uncompromising vitality all its own.

The raging darkness had torn in his soul a lesion that had never healed. For seven long years, the taint had polluted him, erupting with terrible regularity into berserker fury that washed everything human from him. He had fought, Lord how he had fought against those waves of rage and passion. He knew he couldn't fight the tide much longer.

He remembered nothing from the past to account for the disease, could not recall having been bitten or scratched by a werewolf. But from where had the igniting spark come? His life until the onset of the illness had been that of an ordinary man who never thought of himself as overtly cruel or vicious. He didn't feel so even now, though he had to concede that he must have killed hundreds of people. The one possible cause—that he was simply destined to lycanthropia—was an explanation as unsatisfactory to him as, no doubt, was his victims' consolation that they were born to be slaughtered.

The first clear thought to penetrate the veil of numb perplexity that descended over him when he'd first realized the full extent of his illness was the recognition that he still had the choice of free will. Choice, he had thought bitterly. Free will. The bitterness returned to him now, like a memory of better times best forgotten but stubbornly insistent. The longer it remained, the more it bit into him. Yes, he thought, I have the choice to be just where I want to be when I completely lose my volition.

Time had not dulled his feelings but merely made the dichotomy between his apparent freedom and the thrall of his condition more poignant. His independence had freed him from all the things he'd once thought so necessary and from the ties and the patterns of thought that once had been as important as things. Divorced from his former existence, he no longer filled his mind with details of what he should or could be, but rather with what he was.

But with all of his apparent liberty, he was never really free. Each month he became a wild, killing thing out of control and out of touch with himself, and the situation extended to other levels, as well. If he had the freedom to travel, he also had the necessity to do so. To linger would be to invite capture. And, the transitory nature of his career across the continent guaranteed a life without companionship.

Such thoughts had bothered him more at first, when he was still reacting strongly to the death of his girlfriend, the first of his victims. More difficult to contemplate was the extent of his crimes. After all, he was a vicious, bloody killer. Only the fact that he never remembered his depraved acts managed to palliate him.

The slight breeze subsided and the air warmed. In the tree, a pair of birds frolicked and chirped, and while half of him wanted to tear them apart, the other half relaxed at their song. Soon he dozed fitfully. In his sleep, he dreamed of a place where scintillating lights shone all around him and there was a sound that pulsed with his blood.

As he walked through this place, he realized he no longer was bent and warped but strode straight and tall. The lights around him diffused and merged with the air until the air itself shone. Ahead, through the shimmering atmosphere, he saw movement that became recognizable as an approaching figure. The figure was on the other side of a doorway that stood by itself on the lustrous plain. The closer he approached, the nearer the figure came. He grew apprehensive, for in the sheen of his surroundings, only the approaching figure was dark.

The figure hobbled toward him in an ungainly manner. At last, he was close enough to see that it was a shocking abomination, a wretched parody of a man become beast. He stopped before the doorway, the figure standing just on the other side. It was difficult to face the thing, all hairy, growling, slavering. Worst of all was the expression in its eyes: a combination of hatred and loss that tore at his own remorse and filled him with loathing.

He raised his hand to shield his eyes from the sight and caught a sudden movement. In quick panic, he realized the creature had also raised its hand, and fearful of being struck, he lashed out. His fist smote a hard, flat surface, and the surface shattered with dreamy slowness, shards fluttering like leaves out of the frame and landing around his feet. He looked dumbly at the empty frame, then to the ground. Each of the broken pieces showed an image of the beast. Blood from a cut on his hand dripped onto one of them.

Hunger woke him, hunger growing as the beginning of the dusk grew. It gnawed deep inside him like a life writhing to escape. His last remaining shred of determination vanished as the hunger waxed like a ball of cold fire in his gut, refusing to go unfulfilled. He fought the tautening of his back and shoulders that hunched him over and drew his head back, chin up, and though his will was strong, the change was stronger. A cracked cry escaped his lips, and convulsions wracked and twisted him into a shape no longer even half-human.

The hunger was incandescent as it seared through his anguished inability to dominate his suffering, to make the hot ravening a thing of cold beauty. As awareness slumped beneath the sensate level, his sight gazed across a seething gulf, through narrowed slits of eyes, searching. Slowly the convulsions ceased, but even before they fully had, his figure moved with quiet, lithe power away from the tree, across a small field, and into a sparsely wooded tract.

Nostrils flaring at the caressing scents of early night, the werewolf stalked countryside that, had he cared to know, was the inland edge of a coastal prairie. After some minutes at an easy trot, he crossed a small, brackish stream at whose banks he paused, sniffing cautiously. The water held a musky odor that hinted at something disquieting.

He leapt over it and ran on, but the disturbing scent clung to his fur and lingered around him. He snarled and snapped at the air and ran faster until he raced across the ground. Soon he left the odor behind, but before he had, he'd already forgotten it in the wild exaltation of his run. Another smell finally brought him up short—the scent of humans. The lights from a small settlement shone fitfully through the trees. Circling until he was downwind from any dogs the settlement might have, he carefully approached the nearest houses.

His wild run left him with a ravening more rampant than before, but he didn't let it interfere with his caution. He prowled around for some time, noting where there were dogs and where he would be free to move as he wished. Then he heard a nearby door open and the sound of voices. He crept closer, heard the door bang shut. Peering through a bush, he saw a young man, good food full of vital energy, walking down the street.

Three blocks later, the werewolf leapt and slashed, reveling in the waves of suffering and fear that flooded over him.

The reek of blood, sweat, and terror mingled pleasingly in his sensitive nostrils. The young man staggered back, moaning loudly, but the werewolf did not give him a chance to cry out. He sprang and sank his fangs into the quivering throat, ripped with a savage shake of his head, and drank deeply. The body in his clutch twitched and jerked then lay still. The tang of blood mixed easily with the dying scents of sweat and fear.

He dragged the body away from the houses and into the weeds of a field not far from the settlement. There he devoured part of the corpse. When he had filled his belly, he scuffed a shallow depression in the dirt of the field and, dog-like, buried the remains.

Later, as he loped across empty, misty fields beyond the settlement, he shrieked a howl of delight at his power. Had he, in his more lucid self, been near enough to hear that howl, he would have been struck not by the power of the cry but by its haunted, lonely quality.

He raced, the wind breezing past his ears. His snout lifted again to howl when a disturbing scent wafted across his path, and he halted in a sudden confusion of misplaced steps and heartbeats.

Something was near in whose smell a correspondence to the odor of blood was unmistakable. Yet he was not immediately impelled to pursuit as he usually would have been. Often he had killed wantonly, long after his belly was full and his hunger sated, especially in such locations as this, where he could take time to tease and tear. Why he hesitated this time was not clear, only that some quality of the smell caused fear to spear though him.

He sniffed cautiously to find the scent's direction. Hatred cut through the apprehension and prodded him in the direction of the smell. Padding along uneasily, he tracked the wind-borne scent. The closer he seemed to get, the more overpowering the smell became, engendering a ferocity he felt only when slaughtering his prey and, at the same time, causing an awful, sickly sweet taste to rise out of the back of his throat.

The trot became a rangy run as hatred and gorge rose. Air came and went heavily through his lungs, his tongue lolled out of his mouth. Then his feet splashed into brackish water. He stumbled onward for several steps, slowing to a stop. The water was saturated with the odor he had been chasing, and his heaving breath gave him no respite from it. Lurching, he sloshed out of the water onto dry ground.

The overwhelming musk permeated the air, and he became aware that the scent was only borne by the water but was not of it. The smell surged as if its source approached. He hunched down, afraid. The fear became a pain that jerked a grunt from his throat and doubled him over.

His stomach trembled; nausea rose in his throat. For many minutes, he crouched, chest a shuddering bellows. He desperately wanted to run, to escape the pungency drowning him in its excess, but the sick weakness drained his limbs. He could do no more than straighten on shaking legs.

As he raised his eyes to view the source of his misery, he beheld a waif-like female. Her pale, naked skin glowed opalescent in the moonlight. Lank hair the color of yellow-green straw draped over her shoulders and small breasts and cascaded down the shallow curve at the small of her back. She had a pointed chin, high cheekbones, and eyes like small circles of night with a star aglitter in each. Creasing her face was a splash of a smile, at once mocking and beckoning as it drew colorless lips back from tiny, even teeth. One hand reached up to entwine the cascade of hair. Ripples and waves played down its length. The other hand stretched out toward him, fingers flexed, palm upward. She bent closer, the extended hand sliding beneath his muzzle, stroking. The black pits of her eyes held his gaze, drawing him into their depths.

Then waves of hunger cut through his fear, hunger more devastating than any he'd known before. Slaver drooled from his jaw into the palm of her hand as she continued to stroke him. Rage washed across his sight, blurred her image in a vision of rent flesh and torrents of fear feeding his empty passion.

He coiled the steel of his muscles, tried to calm the quaver in his gut. Still she stroked beneath his hideously dentated slaughterhouse mouth. Still she gazed steadily into his eyes. Then a twinkle of laughter terrible in its derision trickled from her throat. The throat he would rip and tear to shreds! He leapt with all the power at his demonic command.

A whirling wisp of hair brushed gently across his eyes as his fangs tore emptiness, as his throat gulped salty air. The music of her ridicule filled his head. He saw her standing ten feet away, and again he sprang and missed. Then he pursued her across the field and into the night, but she was always a whirling, fleeting wraith one step beyond his seizure.

Taunting, she ran him until she finally disappeared into the mists of the last hour before dawn. Pain wracked him as his metamorphosis eviscerated his beast yet denied him completely human form. Dawn spread across the sky by the time he'd found a safe place to hide for the coming day, and the first rays of the sun saw him huddled in the mouth of a drainage pipe beneath a country road.

As the sun rose, it gradually burned off the mist, and by mid-morning, a shaft of its light speared into the pipe's mouth, illuminating the man–beast's form. Shadows in his twilight sleep elicited a small groan from deep inside him, and he stirred uneasily then woke.

Even in his half-formed debilitation, hunger rose preeminently. He rolled onto his belly, arms brought tight against his chest, fist clenched. Elbows scraped against the concrete while he gnawed at the knuckles of his left hand. Gradually, as the pain of desire subsided, weakness came and laved the lesion that's abyss was a well from which nothing could be drawn. He slumped to the bottom of the pipe, cheek pressed against the cool cement.

After many minutes, he lifted his head and crawled out. A pool of water stagnated beneath the lip of the pipe, and it refreshed him a little as he flopped through it. When he reached the other side, he nestled in the tall weeds at the foot of the steep road embankment. He could hear an occasional car pass by, but the slope and the weeds obscured him from view. Curling into a ball, he lay still. His clothes were nearly gone by now, their remains tattered about him like limp pennants. Water from the pool dripped off his fur, soaking into the ground.

The dampened earth seemed to draw him, too, with comforting pressure, and his numbed mind welcomed the firm foundation. But as he lay there quietly, he began to feel restless and uncomfortable, as if something shifted within him, depriving him of the stability he so needed. When he rolled onto his back, the discomfort ceased, as if in turning he had revolved around a center within himself. It was the center that was restless, ungrounded.

He lay there, focusing his attention on that center, tried to hold it still, but something moved and the center moved and, when it did, he moved. But as soon as he had, he could feel the shifting again. Again he tried not to move, tried to hold the center firm, but it would not be held and gradually twisted from his mental grasp. Still he held his body rigid, feeling the center wring within him until the sensation was intolerable, until sanity could bear no more.

A cry made savage by his half-bestial state slashed from his throat, and with terrible effort, he lurched to his feet. Back twisted awkwardly, arms flailing, he thrashed through the weeds and tall grasses at the bottom of the embankment.

Crazed and reeling, he hobbled for a hundred feet, trailing a ragged swath, before he stepped into a depression and pitched headlong to the ground. Pounding heart a counterpoint to panting breath, he lay there, confusion clouding his thoughts.

What was this sensation? He could feel it this very moment, urging him to motion, any motion, pulling part of him at odd angles to the rest. He rolled onto his stomach, wanting to lie quietly, to be drawn to the substantial Earth, to feel its security. Instead, he felt perched on the edge of an abyss into which he was gradually slipping.

As he struggled to understand his plight, he suddenly recognized that part of the force must be gravity. He could feel its attraction as he lay there, with his ear pressed to the ground. It held him with firm embrace, pulled him straight to its own center, inexorably defining up and down. So why was he groveling on the ground, torn inside at odd angles? He could feel within himself, just beneath his rationalization, another force, an oblique attraction, compelling him to motion, tugging sideways, twisting as it tugged.

He puzzled over it for some time before he realized that the conflicting force must also be gravity—that of the moon, the orb that's penultimate brilliance brought his darkest night. He had no doubt about it now that he had intuited this fact. Earth's gravitation drew his body, while the Luna's lured his reason into opposition.

But gravity was always present in life. Earth and the moon were always there, always pulling, even when he wasn't in the throes of his sickness. If simple gravity were at fault, wouldn't he always be a ravening, wild werewolf? Wouldn't other people be likewise? Gravity was part of the answer, but where the rest lay he was, at present, too exhausted to ponder. He closed his eyes and slept a shallow sleep troubled not by dreams but by visions of equations and vast energies feeding more numbers into the system.

Hours later, he woke. Groaning, he shifted onto his back. A breeze rustled the weeds around him. Thoughts from earlier in the day filtered into his consciousness.

He knew that gravity alone could not account for his condition, for it was a constant factor applying energies at every moment. Only his sensitivity made him different from other people. He rolled over. True, gravitational force did seem to have an effect, but moonlight must be the controlling element. His metamorphosis, his voracious hunger, occurred at no other time but that of the three days of the full moon.

He turned onto his side, pillowing his head on his arm. But why? That these reactions actually occurred he could no longer deny, but what was the underlying mechanism of the enthrallment? There must be an element inherent in moonlight that triggered a natural reaction in himself, some characteristic or frequency that resonated with a like characteristic. He could think of only one difference between moonlight and other kinds of light: The moon shone by reflection rather than by its own illumination.

The pain of transformation began to stiffen his back and work its way through his shoulders. The sun was low in the sky, and soon dusk and the moon would bring the change. He welcomed it for the release it brought, though it would be the last metamorphosis he would have to suffer this time. The full moon was waning, and as it did, its influence weakened. Tomorrow night he would be sick to death, but at least he would not change. Now, though, the cramping was building, making thought difficult.

He realized then that he was parched, and he scrabbled through the weeds to the stagnant pool. The water had a nasty taste, but it soothed his dry throat. As he lay down by the pool, trying to organize his thoughts, his consciousness became more disassociated by the minute.

He was thinking of...reflected light. Light and gravities, and the way they tore him in different directions. Why couldn't he pull them together into something comprehensible? He felt the urge to move, but discovered he could not. Weakly he lifted an arm, let it fall back to his chest. Then the change twisted something inside him that refused to move, and darkness slipped over his consciousness as flood waters inundate a countryside.

The sigh he drew as he opened his eyes echoed raspingly deep in his chest, emerged as a rumbling growl. Rising, he began to hunt. Across several miles of fields he ran in a lazy lope that rapidly covered the ground. His course rambled due to the many smells he caught drifts of in his nostrils. Over all was the unmistakable odor of ocean, but cutting through even the tang of brine came a smell unpleasing in a musty way. It was a smell familiar to him, but he could not remember where he'd encountered it before.

The odor grew sharper the farther he progressed, so he tacked across the wind currents to avoid it. It seemed, though, that the more he tacked, the stronger the smell became. He cut back across his own path and headed in the opposite direction.

The ploy didn't work; the smell was more intense than ever. Worse, the odor brought his ever-present hunger to even greater intensities. Soon he was foaming at the mouth with desire for satiation. Slaver drooled and dried into white streaks on the fur of his chest.

Then, abruptly, the musk was gone, as if it simply dissipated into the atmosphere, and human spoor flooded his nostrils. He could tell he was on the verge of a small town, and the presence of so many people increased the nervousness brought on by the now-vanished odor.

He slunk through an outlying neighborhood, arousing a few resident dogs with his scent, but he was too hungry for his usual circumspection. Finally, in desperate need, he attacked a thick, middle-aged woman as she emerged from a car on a dark street. He allowed her no sound; she took but a moment to die. After feeding hastily where he'd killed, he left the body where it lay and ran to the edge of the neighborhood and across a field to a small stand of trees.

For reasons he could not recognize, he felt uneasy, as if eyes other than his own had taken in the sight of his kill. He stopped in sudden suspicion, snuffing at the light breeze. Scents from various small animals hovered on the currents, and everywhere was the briny smell of nearby ocean.

A thought flittered small and dark with a tiny glitter across his mind. A gossamer lighted on his face, clung for an instant to his muzzle, then whisked away as he batted at it in a disconcerted rush. Uneasiness twisted coldly in his belly. Raising his face to the moon, he howled long and disconsolately, and the rising breeze whiffled away the sound.

Shouts and the sounds of doors slamming came from the houses. A car started, its headlights stabbing on in a blaze that reflected from his eyes as if the orbs were silver emeralds. He hunched there uncomprehendingly for some moments before he realized the car was coming towards the copse where he hid.

Across the next field a larger stand of woods lay dark in the moonlight. Before the car reached the copse, he had entered and gone some distance into the larger stand. Soon he was several miles beyond that, moving rapidly into the sea wind. Even with the danger left behind, he felt tense and couldn't shake the feeling of being watched, though he knew it couldn't be so. He quickened his lope to a fast run.

Running, which usually brought elation and power, this time brought nothing but a sort of dizziness, and the disorientation infuriated him all the more. Snarling and snapping at the air, he tore at imaginary flesh, rending it with savage jaws, tossing the phantom pieces from him with wild shakes of his head. But try as he might, he could not recapture the joys of mutilation and slaughter.

Soon the snapping stopped, and he simply ran, dread looming over fading memories of delight. He lost all thought of direction, all caution, and so it was with startled surprise that he felt himself splash into knee-deep water. His feet sank into thick muck at the bottom, and losing his balance, he stumbled and fell full length. A great gout of brine gushed into his mouth and up his snout.

As he floundered, choking and confused, to his feet, the dread odor reached out, insinuated itself around him, clung tenaciously to his fur. Its sudden potency made him reel. Batting weakly at the surrounding air and shaking his head flaccidly, he tottered to firmer ground and tried to escape the smell. But wherever he turned the smell was stronger, denser.

He wavered, then crashed to his knees. His chin dropped to his chest as he slumped to his haunches, gnarled, clawed hands lying in his lap. Then she was in front of him, and his black rage wanted to rip her slight body, fling her, stomp her, splash the ground with her blood. But the weakness in his gut was too overwhelming. His stomach trembled, grew tight, loosened, and in spasmodic heaves, regurgitated its gory contents.

Though he tried to stop, he finally spewed up the last of it. Then he collapsed to his side, panting. Her laughter twinkled in the dark air. The rustling sound as she approached caused him to flinch back, but in his weakness, he could not move far. As she squatted and put out a hand to stroke his forehead, he wrapped feeble fingers around her ankle.

She seemed not to notice his advance, and he craftily closed the claws into a circlet and concentrated his eviscerated power on holding the ankle. She would not escape him this time. Then, disconcertingly, she bent close and blew a teasingly light breath in his ear, her yellow-green hair cascading over his eyes and muzzle.

With a snarl, he jerked her ankle toward him and snatched up to entwine the claws of his other hand in the fall of her hair. But there was no ankle to grasp, only a whisk of damp air, and her hair trickled though his fingers like a splash of water. He heaved himself to his feet, where he wobbled dizzily. She was there, just beyond the limits of his vision. He cast about with his eyes, his sense of smell, but her odor was as pervasive as the night, and both hid her from him.

Slashing at the air with his talons, he thrashed into the darkness, grasping, reaching, flinging himself around and around until confused senses brought him to a staggering halt. As if from nowhere her hand caressed his arm, and he struck savagely as her mirth twittered in his ear. Then she tugged at the fur on his chest, and he lunged after her.

He still could not see her, but as she moved, her scent became less pervasive, more directional. Trying to calm the excited heaving of his chest, he followed in her wake as rapidly as he could. She led him across a hundred yards of marshy land, and as the ground underfoot grew steadily firmer, her speed increased. Soon he had to run as fast as possible to keep pace.

Even his insatiable desire for her flesh was forgotten in his mad rush. They ran for miles, her course shifting and changing, he hounding her trail and gradually falling behind. Soon her odor was a mere drift on the prevailing ocean breeze. He was near enough that his sensitive ears could just barely perceive the sound of distant surf.

His hunger for the girl blossomed again, and he sprang forward, following her diminishing spoor. Ahead was the glitter of lights and neon, and he knew danger lay in that direction, but that was the way she had gone, so he followed.

Sounds reached his ears, and the deeply buried human part of him recognized them as music and laughter. He followed the girl's scent until he halted just outside the circle of lights around the building from which the music came. Several people loitered in the parking lot, leaning on cars, while others came and went through the open doors. A pickup truck pulled into the parking lot and stopped beneath the neon sign. The music was loud, and he crouched, half-entranced by it, half-confused as to what to do. The girl's trail led out into the shining light where he dared not follow.

Then her touch brushed his shoulder. He whirled in a flash, and there she was, only a yard away. He need only leap and slash, but she turned from his attack with easy grace. Fury blew up inside him like a balloon of fire, glazing his vision. He turned after her, slashed, missed, slashed again, but could not quite touch her.

As she tripped lightly away, he threw himself after her, body and soul bent on her destruction, but he was always too late. A wisp of hair, the breath of her movements, the titter of her mirth were all he could catch. The hot boil within blinded him as he whirled after her, his world spinning in crazed desire and ravenous need. Turning, he rushed, pivoted, rushed, and always she eluded his thrashing arms, his clutching talons. Then, abruptly, she broke from their dance—broke and ran straight from him.

It was the moment of panicked flight that all predators look for, and as he sprang after her, she faltered and stumbled. He knew he had her, knew that his monstrous speed and power would descend on her frailty before she could recover. With a terrible roar, he leapt straight at her.

29

But she was not there, and suddenly he was in the light, and people were all around him screaming, shouting. A car pulling into the parking lot transfixed him in the blinding stare of its headlights. Panic stricken, he wavered, not knowing what to do. Dimly, beyond the headlights' glare, he could see the people.

There was a sudden motion and something hard struck his chest. More things, rocks and bottles and cans, began to pelt him. Covering his head with his arms, he lunged one way then another, trying to escape this circle of fear. The shouts of the humans grew more predatory, and behind them, he heard a metallic snicking sound that was almost familiar. A moment later something slammed into his right shoulder and ripped its way though him as a simultaneous explosion crashed in the air.

He staggered backwards with the shock, and another bullet whizzed by his head. Throwing himself sideways through a veil of people who recoiled from him, he charged out of the light. A third bullet followed him into the darkness, tearing a chunk out of his side, just below the injured shoulder. The sounds of the humans faded as he fled, but her laughter chased him across black sandy fields of coarse shore scrub.

He knew she was following him, that if he stopped and turned, she would be right there. But he had no stomach for her now. His only thought was of escape, escape from her and this area where humans would hunt him with dogs at first light of day.

The injured arm didn't pain him much as he clasped it across his body with his good hand, but the wound in his side shot fire through his chest with every breath, every jolting step. He wanted to stop, rest, lick his wounds, but the danger that would follow urged him on. The girl's musk came up on him as he ran, and he heard the soft pad of her feet following close on his heels. She giggled and poked the small of his back.

Prodded, he increased his speed, but the loss of blood, pain, and confusion made him weak. She poked again, harder, and he stumbled to the sandy ground, chest heaving. Blood began to spread a dark stain on the sandy earth beneath the injured shoulder and side. He could smell its salt finding secret union with the briny air. She stood over his supine form, her light laughter mocking his weakness.

How long he lay there he could not tell, but presently he heard the faint bay and bark of dogs coming from beyond the girl's mirth. The hunters had not waited until morning. They were coming now.

He tried to rise, but the girl pushed him, and he fell back to the ground. He crawled weakly away, staggered to his feet facing her, and whimpered. She giggled. The dogs were closer now, close on the scent of his trail. He saw the dancing and bobbing of lights as the people followed the dogs toward him. He turned and ran. Just ahead sounded surf, and he tottered onto the beach with his pursuers less than a quarter of a mile behind.

Down the moonlit strand he ran, his shadow chasing him, the girl behind that, the humans and dogs approaching rapidly. As his wounds sapped his strength, dizziness saturated him, and finally he let his arm fall to his side. Blood dripped from his fingers, black in the silver light. The soft sand shifted queasily beneath his feet, slowing his run to a nightmarish flounder.

He threw a glance over his shoulder and saw the pursuing lights turn onto the beach. The barking dogs began baying with the immediacy of his scent and blood, and a moment later came a shout as one of the men spotted him. Shots sounded in the night air, and bullets whistled by him. The girl was so close he could feel her dank breath on his neck. His own breathing came hard. Her hair tangled around his head, their limbs seemed to be running together.

Terror tightened in his gut. Then she was on his back, bearing him to the sand.

He fell, and a wave washed against them, throwing spray into the air. A titanic heave threw her off, and he lurched to his feet. The pursuers were almost on him now, and the only escape was out, into the water.

Leaning into the current and waves, he forced his way past the breakers. The surge of the waves alternated with a strong undertow, and he had to struggle to keep his footing. Turning, he could see his pursuers casting aimlessly around the moonlit beach for a trace of him. Their lights blazed across the water, but now he was beyond their reach.

He saw the girl standing in the midst of the breakers, her pale body glistening in the moon's opalescent glow, her smile gleaming. Then she dipped beneath the waves and disappeared. He stood, fur plastered wetly to his forehead, afraid.

The sand beneath his feet shifted in the current's ebb and flow. Fingers of undertow insinuated through his fur and wrapped around his legs. The pull of the water grew stronger. The werewolf lifted his face to the moon and howled. Then the sand beneath him gave way. Arms flailing, he kicked out, but he was weak and the water too powerful for all its insubstantiality, and he could no longer resist it. Equilibrium completely lost, he kicked out again, wavered for one pulse beat, then silently slipped beneath the waves.

VENDO-SPENDO

HE WAS WALKING DOWN A city street. It was morning, but it felt like afternoon.

"Vending, oh! Spending, oh! Oh so ready for the sending, oh!"

What was it? A whole block? It was certainly that, larger than any structures nearby. Big and square and black. No windows. No doors. No features. One big, square, black, smooth, windowless building.

"Vending, oh! Spending, oh! Juicy ripe for the blending, oh!"

Looking up, looking down, looking all around, he couldn't tell from where the voice wafted. Or the smell. The smell was strong and of sweets and other good goodies to eat. Both the nonsense rhyme and the smell had assaulted him simultaneously, and he certainly was hungry. Follow the rhyme, reasoned he, find the food; they seemed to drift the same currents.

"Vending, oh! Spending, oh! Now so ready for the bending, oh!"

The corner ahead spewed forth voice and odor in audible, smellable tangibility. No, not corner. Alley. A small, dark alley. It was only a few...

"Vending, oh!"

...more...

"Spending, oh!"

...steps...

"Juicy sweet for the…"

…round the corner…

"…rending, oh, how are you?"

…to see this crooked little man in a shabby old tux sitting on dirty pavement, smile slitting his head ear to ear, back against smooth, black wall, hands folded across a bulging cloth bag in his lap. An upended top hat sat next to him like a beggar's repository. His split mouth was full of dirty yellow teeth, but his pointy black shoes were polished spit and shine.

So were his eyes.

One hand moved to topper, one gripped bag, and he slithered standing, his back still braced against the black, smooth wall like he was attached. He bowed, sweeping topper beneath arched belly, rose, sat topper on top.

"Here!" He thrust out the bulging cloth bag.

"Here!" He pointed to the unbeforeseen door in the smooth, black wall.

"Here!" The cloth bag again, greasy smile still plastered to parchment face.

"What…?"

"Moolah, boy! Bag of dough! Here!"

It clinked unlike any bag of bread he'd ever had before, and so it was that a fatal, unthinking curiosity aimed his clutch.

"What the hell," he said as he grabbed the bag.

"What the hell!" he yelled then, but too late.

Proverbial drowning man clutching at proverbial camel humps, he grabbed at the twin tails of Topper's tux, only to find shredding cheesecloth as the mouth of the door in the black, smooth wall gulped and swallowed him.

A snicker slid snidely through the crack in the door before it closed.

"Not quite as dark in here as out there," was his first reaction to the long, long, long fluorescently lit corridor.-

Gleaming smooth tiles—white—were floor. Pockmarked tiles—also white—sound-proofed the ceiling.

"Mighty fine," he thought then, looking at the double row of vending machines lining the corridor walls.

"Mighty fine!" he thought, looking at his bag of moolah. His bread.

"What'll it be?" he questioned himself. "Could be anything. The future's wide open. Mmm mmmm," browsing the walls. "How about a candy and soda?"

Extracting the appropriate coinage from the bag presented no problem. Neither did extracting the yummies: The directions were perfectly clear. The wrappers were a bit more difficult. For them there were no directions, but he managed to manage.

Yummy!

Yummy, yummy, yummy.

"How about some gummy?" queried he of himself. How about it! He grinned, groped for change, plopped it into a machine. A neon sign on the machine lit up, saying: "More."

More? Inflation. Sure. Got lots! He plopped in more. Chicka-chicka-chick. Kerchunk! Gum-gum the gum. Yum!

What about the empty wrappers and soda can? Ah!

Flashing neon spelled "Put it here!" in red and blue above a white receptacle. No sweat. Now to explore. He hefted the dough bag. Not much bread in it, but sure are a lot of yummies! He grinned and trotted off, down the hall, future silver flashing in his smile.

Thirty steps brought him to a door. Said "Entrance" on it. Thirty steps more beyond "Entrance" was another "En-trance," and so on down the corridor, until the end, where at left right angles, there was another corridor. Full of vending machines, all bright, colorful, shiny, and glowing neon nimbuses.

"Whoop-te-doo!" He galumphed on down the hall, looking for the dream machine of promise, ignoring the "Entrances" along the way until he tired after a turn or two onto more halls of colorful neon assurances, and settled down for a soda and a smoke. Coins click, Soda and smokes chicka-chicked. Slurp, puff, slurp, puff, slurp, puff, slurp-puff, slurp-puff, slurpuff, slurpuff, slurpuff! And more rational this time. Up and off, but not wildly. Up and trash in "Put it here!" and tried the next "Entrance."

Opened the "Entrance" door, stepped through, and as it slammed shut behind, saw fluorotubes, saw white tiles floor and ceiling, saw vending machines. A gulp and sweat drip later, he turned back to the door, but all he saw there was a vending machine selling plastic good-luck pieces.

"Where's the door?" he asked it, receiving in answer a click or two without monetary incentive.

"Holy Jesus!" he swore, but his only answer was a multitudinous click from the whole assemblage.

He really started dripping now. Cold sweat leaked down from his armpits. Crime-in-nee! His sodas were beginning to tell, and he needed to wash his face in cold water. Where's the john?

Twenty minutes later, all was seemingly well as he found the proper door. He pushed through and was faced with one receptacle and thirty machines. They sold combs, hankies, puzzles, prophylactics, toothbrushes, breath drops, nail clippers, key chains, nail-clipping key chains. All sorts of oddities, knickknacks, and safe things were on sale in this emporium. He thought he could ignore them, but he couldn't.

Pay toilet, then at the sink he found that spring-loaded faucet handles permitted no wastage. He could not wash his face and hold the handles, too, so he must buy a hankie to washcloth his face. A toothbrush brushed cloying sweetness from his teeth, and he was ready to return. Refreshed. He found the door out, or back, and jumped through, or in, landing on both feet. Back in the corridor.

Where he wandered for some time.

36

Much later, half a moolah bag later, he was tired. His belly hurt from too many sweets, his feet hurt from too many miles of shiny white tile, and he did not know the time. Vending machines don't sell time.

It had been days though. Must have been. He had slept four times, sprawled on the floors of locked johns, and his beard was beginning to itch. A john machine yielded a razor for four bits after the first sleep, but it was good for only one shave, and since then, he hadn't bought another.

He'd gone up in the world, though. "Entrances" had led to corridors that had led to other corridors. "Entrances" also had led to stairwells that always led up to other corridors that led to more corridors lined with vending machines and "Entrances" that led to other corridors or stairwells that always led up. He couldn't find a return route to the lower levels of this structure where he was sure he could find an exit. Or, at least, that dirty little man with the split yellow grin, pointy black shoes, and black eyes. "Entrance" after "Entrance" he tried, hoping for a down route or exit, but always up he went, or stayed the same.

"What if I try not to stay the same?" he asked the corridor ahead of him. Machine chitters mocked, but he tried just the same.

Odd things he tried. He danced a whirling dervish down the hall. Calisthenics he tried. He'd have kicked a vending machine, but the too many miles of shiny white tile have rendered his feet useless for that. He bought a pack of colored wax crayons and drew obscene pictures and hieroglyphs on the faces of vending machines, trying humanification to no avail. He sketched a hopscotch board in black shoe polish on shiny white tile. Selecting a two-bit piece of specie, he stood at "Go" and proceeded to "Ten" and back to "Go." Then again. And again. Then he only got as far as "Eight" before he realized he was hungry from exertion.

Picking up the two-bit piece of specie, he employed it with others, received true fruition for his efforts, and sat discontentedly munching Snickers and slurping Coke.

"Help!" he shouted. "Help!" he nearly screamed, and the echoes of his cry sifted down corridor after corridor, only to be soaked up by the acoustic tile ceiling. Then he immediately regretted him impetuosity, remembering the two-nights-ago sleep, locked in a pay toilet.

He'd slept, wakened, dozed, wakened, drowsed, and wakened to a soft, slurping, mewling, moaning at the other side of the pay toilet door. Snuffing and scratching, the thing outside tried to get in, tried weakly to smash the door, thumping its attempt to get at him. Amidst the mewling and moaning, he caught one intelligible word slip from slobbery lips.

"Coin."

A dark shape surrounded a glaringly mad eye that peered through the crack at the edge of the door. Fingers tried to edge into the crack, weak and shaking fingers, to rip the obstructing panel from its hinges. The booth shook slightly with its efforts, and he beat on the fingers with the heel of his shoe until the bloody digits retreated to renew bombardment of the door. The whole time, it moaned and grunted with its effort and need. For hours it seemed to go on, until exhausted, hungry, and terrified, he had slipped into a deep pit of soporific tensions. When he awoke, the thing had vanished into the corridors.

He looked around now, terrified that his voice, heard, would bring a whole horde of slurping, mewling things squirming down the white tiles in desperate search of coin, or even—horror!—food!

A half-imagined sound, a vague click from somewhere down the hall, staggered him to his feet and sent him reeling up the corridor and through an "Entrance."

38

Holy Jesus! Another up stair. Up and up. To where? The top. Out through the door at the top of the stair, not easily, not nonchalantly, but bursting through to catch in the act whatever might be there to be caught in the act, but all there was was a vast clicking, snicking language passing around the corridor that stopped abruptly as if caught in the act.

Yes.

This did not bother him, though. The machines were beginning to click more openly and without interest in silver as he wandered this vending infinity, growing evermore, nevermore tired. And hungry. He barely noticed the machine chatter now.

Quarters bought an automated roast beef sandwich with limp, paper lettuce. More procured soda. The sandwich tasted of plaster, rubber, and string, and he threw it on the floor. Then he saw for the first time the other rubbish through which he must have been wandering lately. Garbage lay strewn about. Half-eaten candies lay in puddles of soda, seething a sweet mist that layered the white tiles to obscurity.

Though quite tired, he bent and lifted the remains of the automated cow lying between two layers of holesome, de-enriched bread. He took it to the "Put it here!" but the flashing red and blue neon was dark. The hole was filled to bursting, overflowing onto the floor, where a mound of pitiful, unreheatable leftovers lay.

"Holy Jesus!" he muttered as the dead cow fell to the floor, and the chitter-chatter of machines forced his hands to his ears. Self-inflicted deafness. Then a maniacal laugh rose from his aching guts, spewed forth from his wracked and shuddering body.

"Sweet Jesus!" he screamed, seeing the end, and as he fell to the floor with the other refuse, machine chitter-chatter descended on truly deaf ears.

He lived for awhile longer, a slurping, mewling thing, and then he lay still. The machines gathered around him, gathered him up, gathered him into themselves. Soon a new machine stood at the end of the filed ranks. On its face, a metal plaque read: The Vendo-Spendo Company, Holyoke, Mass.

HAROLD L

"IT LOOKS TO ME LIKE a case of severe concussion." Chief Resident Appleton let the patient's eyelid close. "He's been mumbling but not making much sense. You say you've been treating him for some time, Dr. Winfield?" Appleton brushed veined hands against his white lab coat.

"That's correct," said the other man beside the bed. "Or, rather, he's been coming to see me with a problem he's had for several years. I can't say I managed to do much to treat him."

Winfield shifted his gaze away from Appleton to the man on the bed. His face was pallid, his nostril edges whitened, his breathing shallow. Winfield could see a flickering that indicated eye movement beneath his closed lids. A sleep researcher might call it REM, indicating that the man on the bed was in the midst of a dream. Winfield knew that nightmare might be more accurate.

Poor Harry, he thought as he sighed, turned away from the bed, and went out into the hall, leaving Appleton to give instructions to the nurse. Walking down the hall to the floor lounge, he felt more tired than fifty-six years had a right to feel. In front of the coffee machine, he fumbled a dollar bill into the slot and watched as the dark liquid streamed into a Styrofoam cup. Appleton walked up just as he removed the cup and raised it to his lips.

"Would you care to step into my office?" Appleton indicated the way, and Winfield soon found himself in the chief resident's office. As he sat down, several drops of hot coffee spilled onto his hand. He flicked them off, then took a sip.

"I take it you disagree with the diagnosis of concussion," Appleton said, seating himself behind the desk and leaning back in the chair. "When the police brought in the patient... what's his name...?" Appleton leaned forward and read a form lying on the desk. "Harold Loucks. When Mr. Loucks was admitted to the hospital, he was examined by an emergency team, and they diagnosed concussion. All the symptoms are there— body cold, respiration weak, stunned motor responses."

He looked expectantly at Winfield, who reached forward and set the cup on the corner of Appleton's desk. Then he sat back and ran his fingers through his hair.

"Look at the evidence," Winfield said after a moment. "No marks or bruises on the head, no fracture, no bleeding or internal pressure. In short, no evidence that he has sustained a blow to the head or trauma to the spine. And the harbor patrol team was very explicit. He was unconscious when they found him, and they didn't harm him in transit."

"What about the explosion?" Appleton pointed out. "The officer in charge said there was an explosion."

"That was in the engine room, aft in the ship. Harry was on the bridge. The blast might have shaken the deck, and it certainly would have been loud, but not enough to cause a concussion. Besides, there were several policemen aboard at the time, and the only one who was injured was the one Harry shot."

"You were on the scene?"

"Yes. I was trying to stop Harry before he did something irrevocable. Unfortunately, I couldn't prevent what happened."

"You knew he intended to blow up the ship?"

42

"Oh, no. That wasn't his intention. I can safely say that Harry would never intentionally do anything that might substantially damage the *Harold L.*"

"The *Harold L?*"

"The name of the ship."

Appleton chuckled and leaned forward.

"You mean that the patient has the same name as the ship he accidentally blew up?"

"That's right. Harry believed that the fate of the ship was tied to his own life. That's why he'd never harm it." Winfield picked up the coffee cup and took a couple of sips before returning it to the corner of the desk.

"He believed this just because of the similarity in names?"

Winfield could tell that Appleton was interested despite his apparent readiness to diagnose Harry as merely a dangerous misfit.

Winfield sighed, wondering just how much of the story he should tell Appleton. As administrator of one of the city's largest hospitals, Appleton would have seen most types of cases that can come into a medical facility, but along with that experience would come a certain hardening of attitudes that separated the successful administrator from the patient he was administering to. For such a man, all cases can be diagnosed, if not always treated. Appleton could be trusted to see the facts, but Winfield knew that facts didn't always reveal the truth. He decided to relate the story, if for no other reason than to share his own grief. It was too late for Harry, now, anyway.

"It all started about fifteen years ago, in the shipyards down at the port. At the time, I'd just completed my internship and was working at the Sheraton Clinic."

"Oh, yes. It recently closed, didn't it?"

"About three years ago. Lack of funds. Too bad, really. The port area needs a good, inexpensive clinic. At any rate, the first incident occurred early one afternoon." Winfield paused and gulped down the rest of his coffee, reflecting that he'd probably want more before long. He dropped the cup into the trash and continued.

"Harry was working on the forward deck of the *Harold L*...."

"Excuse me," Appleton interrupted. "I just want to know one thing: Does the L stand for Loucks?"

"No," Winfield laughed shortly. "It was named after a board member of the Arlingen Lines, the original owner. The L stands for Lambert.

"The *Harold* was in dry dock after being purchased from the Arlingen Lines. The new owners wanted to spruce it up before launching their venture. Harry had only a couple of more days of work on the ship, and that suited him fine. He'd had just about all the razzing he wanted from his coworkers about the similarity in names.

"A load going overhead from the dock to the hold accidentally dropped. One of the lines snapped, or something. Part of the load struck a glancing blow to Harry's skull. He was lucky that he was only knocked unconscious, though he sustained a rather severe gash to his scalp. If the load had landed more directly, he would have been killed. One of his coworkers rushed to fetch me from the clinic, and by the time I arrived, Harry was beginning to come to and was trying to sit. He was woozy and unstable, and a quick examination showed signs of concussion.

"The wound wasn't dangerous, though because it was a scalp wound, Harry had lost a lot of blood. The paramedic team got him into the ambulance and brought him to the clinic. We had a small, in-patient hospital—a dozen beds in three wards—and I kept Harry under observation for a couple of days. He recovered rapidly, physically, at least, and the stunned feeling and disordered vision vanished completely, though he had some difficulty sleeping."

"All this sounds routine," Appleton said. "But a moment ago, you qualified the patient's health by say he'd recovered physically. Was something disturbing the patient?"

Winfield nodded.

"As I said, he had difficulty sleeping. Nightmares. Though he didn't remember much about them, he did remember one scene vividly. He saw himself lying on the deck of the *Harold*. As he lay there, he sank into the surface of it. Then the deck crew came along and painted him into the deck. No so far-fetched a nightmare considering Harry had been stripping old paint off the deck prior to a fresh painting when the accident occurred."

"What did Harry have to say about this?"

"He was afraid. He said that he thought some of his blood had been painted into the deck."

"And that was fifteen years ago?"

"That's right. About two weeks later, Harry returned to have the stitches removed. He was fit, the wound was healing nicely, and there seemed to be no visual or balance problems, but I could tell he was bothered by something. He'd been having more bad dreams.

"'They're like movies,' he told me. 'Only more real than movies.' He described being able to look all around himself, in every direction at once. All he could see was water, like he was in a boat, though he couldn't see the boat itself. I prescribed a mild sedative, and he left, but a week later he was back."

"More nightmares? More drugs?"

"Neither. He was violently nauseous. For nearly two days his stomach refused to hold anything. I thought he might have food poisoning, but he really had few symptoms—primarily vomiting and dizziness. No fever or abdominal cramping at all. I was on the verge of transferring him to a larger hospital when the attack stopped as suddenly as it began. I didn't know what to make of it, but Harry told me he felt exactly like he was seasick.

"Harry had joined the navy right out of high school, mostly to escape a stultifying home environment. After basic training, he was assigned to a warship, but unfortunately, he invariably got seasick while the ship was at sea. He tried various motions sickness remedies, to no avail. There was nothing for him to do but accept a shore assignment in a naval shipyard, where he worked until his discharge. After his enlistment was up, he got a job in the shipbuilding industry, and he'd been doing that for about eight years when the accident occurred.

"And as far as I could tell, Harry *was* seasick. When the attack subsided, I sent him home, but before another week passed, he was back at the clinic with another complaint. This time, it was something different. I don't suppose it really matters what was bothering him. He came down with practically everything he could after that first concussion. And complaints recurred, particularly the seasickness. The nightmares continued, but became less frightening to him as time passed. I think he began to accept them as just another state of consciousness. As you can imagine, he had a difficult time keeping his job at the port, but that sort of work isn't always regular, anyway, and he was generally a good worker."

"Did you check the patient's lifetime case history? Had he always displayed tendencies toward hypochondria?"

"I checked his history as far as possible, both with his family doctor while he grew up and with navy records. Aside from his predisposition to seasickness, there was no hypochondria mentioned by anyone who'd examined him. Besides, in each case, he displayed symptoms of illness."

"As you well know, Dr. Winfield, it is not unusual for a hypochondriac to display symptoms of one sort or another."

"These weren't just of one sort or another. They were specific, often covert symptoms that only a doctor would

46

recognize or lab tests reveal. For example, he came to see me with what, at first, appeared to be a classic case of infectious mononucleosis. All the symptoms were there, and after examining him and performing a few tests, I determined that he did, in fact, have mono."

"Well, if he actually had mono, what was the problem?"

"He didn't have mono. In three days, the symptoms cleared up and vanished."

Appleton laughed, leaned back in his chair, and put his hands behind his head. "Obviously, Harry didn't have mono, so the disorder must have been psychosomatic."

"But you know as well as I that even hypochondriac patients don't display the totality of symptoms, including the hidden ones, for a given disorder or disease. Harry would show all the symptoms, even as far as contaminated blood samples, then whatever was wrong would vanish."

"Are you saying that Harry could have mono, and at the same time not have it?"

"Not exactly. The case was more that he would have mono, or something else, and then he would simply not have it. The duration of the symptoms, whatever the diagnosis, was never regular, even as far as the diagnosed ailment was concerned. Like mono clearing up in three days. For example, he would begin to develop symptoms of the flu for several hours, the symptoms would vanish, and he'd be all right. Or he'd have a cut that refused to heal for a month."

Appleton shook his head, still smiling. "Psychosomatic. It has to be psychosomatic."

"That's what I thought at first. It was Harry who put me on the right track."

"Which was that Harry was psychically linked to the ship, and that whatever happened to the ship was reflected in his own body through illness."

Winfield sighed, relieved that Appleton was taking the story well enough, even if he wasn't believing it. At least he hadn't thrown Winfield out. Perhaps he could get Appleton to believe and use his influence to save Harry.

"That's right. Harry was the first to suspect, and after a time, he confided his suspicions to me. Of course, I didn't let only Harry convince me. I sought other evidence. Unknown to Harry, I checked up on the ship. It had been built by the Arlingen Lines, and for many years it plied a regular route for them along the eastern coasts of the Americas. Then it was sold to a group of investors from the Midwest with no experience in shipping. It was at this time, during the refurbishing of the ship, that Harry's initial accident occurred.

"The investors hired one captain after another and ran a similar route to the one the ship always ran, but they couldn't seem to make their venture pay off. For several years, the ship barely broke even, then it began to lose money. Its condition deteriorated, and the quality of the captains and crews declined. Finally, seven years ago, the ship was sold to Gerold Bryan, the last captain hired by the investment group. Talk around the port was that he was a hard, humorless man who tends to drive a crew and ship to their limits.

"Since Bryan took over as captain, and even more so since he became owner, Harry's problems have increased drastically. I've been treating him as often as twice a week for various maladies. One of the latest was a severe ache just above the lumbar region. That began nearly a year ago, about the time Bryan put into port to have the *Harold* repainted. I suspect he covertly raised the Plimsoll line."

"Why, Dr. Winfield," chided Appleton. "You sound as if you believe this correspondence is real."

"There is more to the story," Winfield said. Appleton waved him on, a tolerant smile on his face. "I guess there were two incidents that convinced me. The first occurred while I was still with the clinic. Harry had been seeing me about abdominal cramping, and I was treating him as an outpatient. He was supposed to return to the clinic the following day, but he didn't show up. I became concerned as the afternoon passed, and when he still hadn't come in by the end of my shift, I went to his apartment.

"He didn't respond to my knock. His landlady said she hadn't seen him all day and didn't think he was in. Knowing I was Harry's doctor, she let me in with her passkey when I told her Harry had failed to show up for an appointment. We found Harry in bed, in a state much like syncope, though with no evidence of cerebral anemia or any other cause for the condition.

"While the landlady called an ambulance, I examined Harry and thought about his belief that he was connected to the ship. After the ambulance arrived and the attendants took him away, I called the offices of the investment group to check on the *Harold*. The company officer I spoke to asked my business, and I said I had a friend on board who had not contacted me. The officer informed me that the *Harold* was experiencing engine difficulties and was floating dead in the water. Repairs would take several days, he said, apologizing for the delay.

"At the hospital, I had Harry fed intravenously while the staff doctors looked him over. They couldn't tell what was wrong, and one was even rather upset at the nonchalant attitude I adopted. Actually, I was not as nonchalant as I seemed but had decided to see if Harry was correct. Sure enough, three days later, Harry regained consciousness, saying he felt like a new man. He was released and went home. Still, I wasn't fully convinced. Part of me believed, but the other part chalked the whole thing up to coincidence.

"The second incident happened when Harry called me late one night. I'd been in my own practice for about a year at the time. Needless to say, Harry was my most frequent patient, though I had long since ceased to charge him for my services. A friendship had developed, and he often came to see me when he was feeling quite well. On this occasion, he sounded distraught and wanted to talk to me immediately. I told him to come right over, but he said no, he wanted to meet me in a bar. Though the hour was late, I knew he was in need of help, so I agreed. He gave me the location, and half an hour later, I sat in a booth across from him.

"I hadn't seen him for perhaps ten days, and he was in bad shape—sallow complexion, sagging features, listless, and already drunk. I urged him to return with me to my office where I could examine him. He refused, then he rambled for several minutes about his connection with the ship. He told me he couldn't sleep, said the ship never stopped moving, "sloshing around," as he put it. Said the only way he could combat it was to get sloshed himself. He had another drink and fell into moroseness for many minutes.

"Then his behavior became overly jovial, as if he was trying to believe that the whole connection thing was a joke, and he had gotten the punch line. He got louder, even a bit obnoxious, which was unusual for him. I begged him to come to my office, but he just wanted another drink. By that time, the waitress said something to the bartender, who came over and told Harry he'd had enough and should go home with me. Harry got angry, and one thing led to another until he had a fight with another customer. Actually, it wasn't much of a fight. Harry was pretty drunk, and after taking a couple of punches, he fell and struck his forehead on a table. The bartender helped me get him to my car, and I drove him to my office.

"The wound was minor, but Harry seemed to have suffered another concussion. I cleaned and bandaged the cut, then put him to bed. In the morning, I asked him to stay around until the next day, and he agreed. In the morning, I phoned the ship's owners again, this time telling them I had minor cargo aboard. Was the ship all right? I was told that during the night the *Harold*'s helm had begun to respond erratically, then the ship had rammed an unknown object and sustained minor bow damage. It would be held up in port once it reached there while repairs were made. After I hung up, I went to see Harry. I related what I'd found out. His eyes were bright when he asked me if I believed him, and I told him I did."

"So," Appleton said. "You actually credit this story?" He leaned forward, elbows on his desk, hands folded in front of him. "I'm sorry, I just don't see that the evidence is more than circumstantial."

"I might think that, too, if I heard the story as I've told it to you. But I watched it unfold, watched is effects on Harry through the years. Perhaps if you could have known Harry, you would understand, too."

"But that's the problem. I didn't know Harry. All I can do is go by the evidence. Anything else is pure conjecture."

"That may be true, but I know that there are cases where the evidence doesn't fit a pre-established pattern. I've witnessed such a case right here in Harry Loucks. You've seen him, Doctor. What would you say is wrong with him?"

"I thought I'd already given my judgment." Appleton sounded a bit testy.

"What you did was determine a few symptoms, and from those diagnose an ailment for which there is no real physical evidence. The real problem with Harry is simply that he is connected in some manner we cannot comprehend to a ship out there in the harbor, and he has been for more than fifteen years."

"Don't you find that a bit preposterous?"

Winfield could tell that Appleton was angry with him, but he really didn't care. His patient and friend was dying in another room in this same building, and there wasn't a thing he could do to stop it. The only hope lay in Appleton believing the story and using his position to influence the

Harbor Authority's ruling. And for this man, that would take a shocking of his own values. Unfortunately, Winfield seemed unable to provide sufficient voltage.

Winfield couldn't blame Appleton, couldn't get mad at him. The story was far-fetched. Besides, he didn't think he'd ever get truly mad again, not since he had spoken with Gerold Bryan about this same matter nearly four years before. The scene came vividly back to him. He had noticed the *Harold L* was due in port, and a few days after it arrived, he went aboard, inquiring after the captain. He knew that Bryan had bought the ship and was owner as well as captain. That was the reason he wanted to speak to the man, to feel him out and perhaps make a plea on Harry's behalf.

Winfield felt the futility of seeking help from Bryan as soon as he entered the cabin. Years as a doctor had taught him to be a fairly accurate judge of character, and clearly, from Bryan's dour, suspicious expression and the curt nod and clipped order dismissing the steward, he was a basically unsympathetic man. Perhaps he was a good captain. Winfield had no way to tell, but he did know that Bryan treated his ship with abuse. He knew this from the conditions he'd been treating Harry for since Bryan's ownership. Bryan would keep the engines running and the hull intact, but the rest of the ship hadn't had an overhaul since he took command.

At the captain's wave, Winfield sat in the single, uncomfortable visitor's chair. Wondering just how to begin, he was silent for a moment, aware that Bryan was staring at him, waiting for him to speak. When he looked up, he was surprised to see resentment buried in the man's gaze. Winfield realized his story had better be good or Bryan would just write him off as a madman. Beginning with the incident of Harry's injury and with his subsequent medical history, Winfield carefully led to Harry's belief that he was connected to the ship.

He watched Bryan while he spoke, and before he'd finished talking, he knew what the man's reaction was going to be. Even after stating that, in his medical opinion, there actually was a psychic correspondence between the man and the ship, Bryan seemed obdurate. Winfield finally stopped talking, feeling foolish at the strain in his voice that must have sounded like weakness to the hard-bitten captain.

Winfield was right about Bryan's reaction, though the captain was not so much outright scornful as mildly derisive. He had obviously not really listened to Winfield after the first couple of comments. None of the evidence had made the slightest impression on his workaday mind.

"What would you like me to do? Stop running the *Harold*? Put it in dry dock for the rest of your patient's life? I'm sorry, doctor, but my entire life savings are invested in this ship, and I don't intend to just throw it all away over some nutcase."

"I'm not asking you to abandon ship, Captain Bryan," Winfield urged. "All I'm asking is that you take extra precautions, that you don't over-work it."

"I have a living to make, and competition is rough. The *Harold* is an old ship, and it must be worked hard to pay for itself. As for its condition, well, frankly, the *Harold* is on it last legs. If you've been following it the way you say you have, you know the original owners worked it for a long time. It has only a few years service left, and I intent to squeeze all the sailing time and cargo capacity I can from it. I'll maintain it as much as necessary, but I don't intend to improve the property."

Winfield started to speak, but Bryan stopped him. "I've often heard you medical men will keep a patient alive long after he should have died, but things are different in the shipping industry. A ship is a vehicle designed to carry cargo across water. It is a tool to be used, not a patient to be pampered. When it can no longer be used, it is discarded, not kept alive through tubes."

"Does use legitimize abuse?" Winfield asked, and Bryan's features grew tight.

"If this Harry Loucks is so interested in the condition of the *Harold*," Bryan said in an edged voice, "then he's welcome to make any improvements he likes. At his expense. I have neither the time nor money to spend on needless cosmetic surgery for a ship that won't outlast the face-lift."

"You'd sacrifice the well-being of another person just be cause you're too lazy and cheap to do otherwise, is that it?"

The question escaped before Winfield could stop himself. Bryan rose out of his chair in anger, but Winfield didn't care. He was angry, too. This blockhead was killing his friend, and he couldn't—no, wouldn't—see the truth.

"I intend to get the most out of my ship," Bryan spat. "And it *is* my ship. I'll run it like I want, and I'll treat it like I want. If you have a crazy patient who thinks he's linked to my ship, well, too goddamn bad. Now," he pointed to the door. "Get out. If I catch you messing around here again, I'll personally take you apart. Understand?"

He roughly thrust Winfield into the corridor, yelling for the steward. When the man arrived, Bryan instructed him to escort Winfield off the ship and to inform the watch not to allow him back on board. Frustration aching through him, Winfield left the ship.

The anger subsided several hours later, when Winfield finally came to terms with the uselessness of the feeling. Even later, when he saw the ship had been painted and suspected the Plimsoll line had been raised so Bryan could carry more cargo than was legal or safe, his anger remained subdued. He had steeled himself to the harshness of the world as personified in Gerold Bryan and gone about the business of trying to find a solution to Harry's problems that would involve neither the *Harold* nor its captain. But now it was too late for Harry. The *Harold* lay holed and partly submerged in the harbor, and Harry lay comatose here in the hospital.

"I'm sorry, Dr. Appleton," Winfield apologized. "I don't mean to sound rude. I'm just worried about my patient."

"I'm aware of the tensions a doctor may experience in connection with a patient, particularly a long-term case," Appleton replied, his anger subsiding. "I suggest we forget the stress of the moment. Please go on with your story. I'll attempt to withhold final judgment until you are finished."

"There really isn't much more to tell. Last week, Harry came to me, saying that the *Harold* was going to be in port. He was excited, almost nervous. I was suspicious of his unusual behavior and asked what the *Harold*'s presence meant to him. He evaded my question, giving a vague statement about retiring and living a life of ease. Superficially, his spirits seemed in better shape than they'd been for several years. Wondering what he had in mind, I asked him to explain, but he just brushed off my inquiry. He left, jovially telling me that the next time he saw me, the visit would be social rather than professional. Worried, I resolved to stop him from committing any foolish acts.

"On the day the *Harold* docked, I was there. I watched all day while cargo was unloaded. By early evening, most of the crew had departed from the ship, I suppose for shore leave. About two hours before midnight, Harry appeared on the wharf. At the time, I was sitting a good distance away, but when I saw him, I stood and walked toward him. As he passed under a light, I could see he had a duffel bag slung over his shoulder. He moved quickly toward the gangplank, and though I called out, he took no notice.

"I was still at least fifty feet away when he went up the gangplank and approached the watch. I called out again, and he must have heard me because the watch was startled by my shouting. Before he could react, Harry pulled a pistol and ordered him off the ship. He saw that Harry meant business and left. As soon as he was on the wharf, Harry cranked the gangplank back and yelled at him to get off the wharf or be shot. The man took me by the arm, though I resisted, and hustled me out of Harry's sight. By this time, Harry was unloosening the mooring cables holding the ship to the wharf. When he dropped the last of them over the side, he disappeared into the interior of the ship.

"I told the watch that he'd better call the harbor police. He nodded and left. A few minutes before he returned, Harry reappeared on the deck, aiming a rifle at half a dozen crew members. I thought I recognized Captain Bryan among the men, but in the dark, I couldn't tell for sure. Harry marched them to the side of the ship, which had, by this time, drifted a couple of yards farther from the wharf. He gestured with the gun, and with audible protests, the men jumped into the slimy harbor water. Harry watched them swim to the pilings of the wharf before he went back into the ship.

"The watch returned as the sailors climbed onto the wharf, and Bryan was indeed among them. As he stood, he saw me, and his eyes lit with recognition. He came over to me, gesturing angrily toward the ship and asking if that was my madman on board.

"I told him that as far as Harry was concerned, he was merely defending himself. Caustically, Bryan said that Harry's defense had better be good, because he was going to call the harbor police. The watch said that he'd already done that. Bryan asked what the hell I was doing here—helping my patient commandeer his ship? Ignoring his sarcasm, I answered that I had been trying to stop Harry from doing anything foolish. Bryan pointed out with a sneer that I hadn't done too well. I had to agree, and more with calculated discourtesy than real anger, I gestured to the ship and pointed out that he wasn't doing too well, either. The ship had drifted several more yards from the wharf, and suddenly there came a muffled rumble as the engines came to life. The ship began to back up.

"Bryan was livid as he turned to me, fists clenched, saying he thought I told him Harry wasn't a sailor. I replied that he wasn't. 'Well, who's running that ship, then?' he asked, waving at the slowly moving bulk as it backed away from the wharf.

One of the crew stepped forward and informed him that Harry still had a man named Jenkins aboard. Bryan cursed and began pacing back and forth nervously, eyes on the ship. I asked the watch who Jenkins was, and he told me Jenkins was the chief engineer.

"A moment later, I heard sirens, and a couple of minutes after, three harbor police cars pulled onto the wharf. Bryan ran over to them as the police emerged, gesturing wildly, shouting, and pointing frequently in my direction. I didn't care what he was telling the police, and I turned to watch the ship. Now it was well away from the wharf and beginning to swing round in a broad arc. The swing stopped and the ship was still for several minutes. Then, with Bryan close behind, one of the police approached me.

"He introduced himself as Lieutenant Thomas and asked if I knew what was going on. Bryan butted in with accusations, but the lieutenant cut him short and asked who I was. I told him I was the personal physician of the man who had hijacked the ship and explained the situation, keeping the details on a clinical level and not admitting my own belief. As I finished, there came a shout from the men on the wharf. The *Harold* had started to move forward.

'What the hell are you going to do?' Bryan bellowed at Thomas. The lieutenant looked at him with barely checked anger and told him that two harbor patrol boats were on their way. Until they arrived, nothing could be done. Cursing, Bryan returned to the edge of the wharf.

"At that moment, a port opened on the *Harold*'s deck level, and two figures stepped through, silhouetted by light. Going to the side of the slowly moving ship, one jumped overboard. The other went back inside. As the man in the water swam ashore, the speed of the ship increased. Bryan was screaming curses at Harry, and one of the policemen went over and told him to keep it quiet. Bryan glared at him but toned down his voice. Then, flashing lights spattered across the dark water as two patrol boats came into sight and sped toward the accelerating ship.

"Everyone crowded to the edge of the wharf to watch the patrol boats pull alongside the moving *Harold*. Thomas stared in the direction the ship was going for a few moments then said that if Harry was trying to get the ship out of the harbor, he was heading in the wrong direction. Instead, the ship was cutting straight across the harbor, and if it wasn't turned soon, it would end up on the far side, in Anderson Cove.

"Anderson Cove, he told me, was once a part of the harbor, before the basin had been dredged for larger ships. It used to have a couple of docks and warehouses alongside, but that the warehouses burned and the docks rotted. After a few years, someone parked a couple of hulks in it, and since then, it had fallen into disuse.

"I realized then what Harry intended to do and told Thomas that Harry was going to try to run aground in the cove. Thomas said he thought the cove was too shallow for a ship the size of the *Harold*. At that moment, Jenkins, the engineer, was helped onto the wharf. He started to say something to Bryan but was interrupted by rising voices from the excited watchers around them.

"The police on the patrol boats had thrown lines to the deck of the *Harold*, and several of them climbed on board. They were having a rough time of it, for by this time, the

58

Harold was moving along rapidly, and the patrol boats bucked and plunged in its wake. Then the boats cast off, and the police ran onto the deck and dropped behind cover. A moment later, faint pops sounded from the ship as someone, we couldn't tell who, fired a gun. There was a pause, then gunfire flared up again. This time I could see flares from the muzzles of the police guns.

"Some of the police began making their way to the superstructure, and one fell to the deck. It seemed as if he'd been hit. The others disappeared inside the ship. Suddenly, the ship lurched and changed direction slightly. Later, I learned that Harry had tried to tie the wheel down with his belt, but that it had apparently slipped after he left the wheelhouse. The *Harold* was, by now, two thirds of the way across the harbor, and I heard Thomas exclaim that if the ship wasn't stopped or turned, it would hit the cove at the edge of its mouth rather than dead center.

"Bryan finished speaking with Jenkins and came over to where we stood. He heard Thomas's statement, screamed cursed in the direction of the ship, then turned back to us, helpless rage distorting his face. Voice shaking, he informed us that Harry had Jenkins fire the boilers to their maximum. Jenkins said that at that rate, they wouldn't last much longer. Thomas told Bryan that everything possible was being done to halt the ship, but Bryan wasn't in a listening mood. He stalked back to the edge of the wharf, resuming his shouted curses.

"By now, everyone on the wharf was spellbound as the ship rapidly closed on the opposite shore. It hit with a dull, crunching thud as it rammed into the left side of the cove's mouth, and the bow was lifted clear by the upward curve of the shallow shore. Water churned furiously at the stern as the engines continued to try to propel the ship ahead but only partially skewed it across the mouth of the cove. As the ship ground to a halt, Bryan danced

59

on the wharf, waving his arms wildly and yelling for the police on board to shut off the engines.

"The two patrol boats pulled alongside the beached ship, and a moment after, the ship shuddered and the crump of an explosion sounded thickly as a hole ripped through the hull near the stern. Great gushes of gray steam billowed out to dissipate rapidly in the night air. A second explosion, more muffled than the first, shook the ship, then water began rushing through the hole, and the stern began to sink, pulling the bow even higher into the air.

"Bryan stood with fists tightly clenched at his sides, shoulders hunched, cursing Harry and muttering about over-fired boilers. He looked at me, rage glazing his eyes. 'I hope you're satisfied,' he grated between clenched teeth. I just stood there, unable to speak. Then he demanded to know what Thomas was going to do about Harry. Thomas told him that Harry would be taken into custody and that the case would be handled by the courts. Bryan began to rail at the court's ineffectiveness, but Thomas stopped him with a curt pardon, turned on his heel, and strode back to his car. Bryan glared after him, then spat on the wharf. He gazed out at the wrecked ship then turned eyes filled with hatred and vengeance on me.

"'I'm going to have the *Harold* salvaged,' he snarled. 'It's going to be taken apart piece by piece.' He laughed meanly. 'Should be interesting to watch your patient while that happens.' Then he turned and went back to the edge of the wharf.

"Dazed at the turn of events, I went over to the police car, where Thomas was speaking over the radio to someone. When he finished, he turned to me and said that Harry had been found in a forward compartment, unconscious but apparently uninjured. The policemen who found him had no explanation for his unconsciousness but positively stated that they were not responsible.

"They brought Harry and the wounded officer over to the wharf on one of the patrol boats, and before the ambulance arrived, I gave both of them a cursory examination. The officer's leg wound was not severe, and while there were no marks or injury on Harry, he remained unconscious. After that, the ambulance came, and the patients were loaded in it and driven here.

"I guess that's all there is," Winfield finished.

"I'd say it seems to have ended well for your patient," Appleton said.

"Well?" Winfield snorted. "Haven't you listened to a thing I've said?"

Appleton's expression was serious as he stood up and came around the desk. He sat on the corner, hands folded in his lap. "As soon as he regains consciousness, he—and you—will see that this is all superstitious nonsense."

"He won't regain consciousness."

"Certainly he will. He must have been knocked out when the ship ran aground, even if there were no signs of trauma. He must also be suffering from shock of some sort. We'll know when he wakes up tomorrow."

"Don't you understand? The ship's a wreck, and it's sticking out into the main channel. I heard Thomas tell Bryan that if Harry had actually made it into Anderson Cover, there would be no possibility of salvage due to the shallow bottom and silting. But where it is, the wreck has got to be moved or dismantled as soon as possible. In fact, they're probably at work already. Don't you see why tomorrow will be too late?"

"I see you're distraught," Appleton soothed, looking with concern at Winfield. "Why don't you go home and rest? When Harry wakes up tomorrow and discovers that the *Harold L* is already torn apart, he'll see the foolishness of believing in some esoteric connection between himself and the ship. And after a good rest, so will you." Appleton extended his hand as Winfield rose and allowed himself to be steered to the door. "You can be sure I'll personally call you when Harry wakes up."

Winfield nodded mutely and went out of Appleton's office. He felt not so much defeated as tired. He hadn't really expected Appleton to believe him. He drove home, went inside, fixed himself a mild sedative, and lay down in bed. Four hours later, he was wakened by the ring of his phone. Groggily, he picked up the receiver. Dr. Appleton was on the line. Would Dr. Winfield please come to the hospital? Yes, the patient was awake, but there were complications. He'd rather not discuss the case over the phone, but let Dr. Winfield see for himself. Winfield told Appleton he'd be right over. He hung, up, dressed, and drove to the hospital. Appleton was in Harry's room when Winfield entered.

"I'm not quite sure what to make of it," Appleton said quietly but urgently. "He's awake, but we're getting signs of renal failure as well as pneumonia. He also has no feeling in his extremities."

"Excuse me for a moment." Winfield stepped closer to the bed, afraid to look. But he knew he had to. Harry's eyes were open, staring at the ceiling. When Winfield came within their range, recognition lit in them, but the light was dull, flickering.

"Hi, Doc."

"Hello, Harry. How do you feel?"

"Huh...not so good." Harry paused, his gaze returning listlessly to the ceiling. He looked back at Winfield. "They said I wrecked the *Harold*." He shook his head sadly. "I don't remember."

Winfield put his hand on Harry's shoulder.

"It's all right, Harry. You don't have to remember, now. Just relax." Winfield began to examine him.

"I feel funny, Doc," Harry said after a few minutes. "Sort of like the time of the fight. I don't really know." He shook his head again and closed his eyes. "I think I was trying to put the *Harold* in Anderson Cove," he said a few moments later. "Is that right?"

"That's what you were trying to do."

Harry closed his eyes, and his features went slack, and seemed to sag even more with each passing moment. Harry was wasting away before Winfield's eyes. Winfield thought Harry had fallen asleep, but then the eyes flickered open. The gaze was unfocused and took several seconds to settle on Winfield. When they did, Winfield was certain that Harry failed to recognize him at first.

"Oh, Doc." Harry's voice was husky with distance. "Do you remember the time in the...." His eyes closed again.

Winfield stepped back from the bed. Appleton was standing close by.

"What do you think?" Appleton asked. "Does this fit the pattern of the patient's illness? What was his mental condition the last time you examined him?"

"As of yesterday he was physically and mentally stable," Winfield replied. "Nothing like this."

"Well," Appleton said, rubbing his chin. "I suspect that there may have been some internal brain injury—a lesion or clot or something. We'd like to run a CAT scan, possibly perform minor exploratory surgery, and you seem to be the closest person to a relative we have. We like permission...."

"Do what you want," Winfield said tersely. "Whatever you do will not make the slightest difference. Harry is dead."

"Ah, yes, the ship again. Well, we'll probably put him in the mental ward on the eighth floor, considering his past history and his present state of apparent mental degeneration. Would you object to that?"

"If I were you," Winfield said, walking to the door, "I'd put him in ICU. By this evening, tomorrow at the latest, there will be a flat EKG followed by massive organ failure. Death will follow. It will be a death that even you will have to accept, Dr. Appleton. Now, if you will excuse me, I don't think I care to witness any more of this."

Appleton nodded sharply, his mouth a stiff line. He turned back to the bed, ordering that patient be taken to the eighth floor. Winfield sighed and left. He took the elevator to street level and went out into the midmorning air. Tired as he was, he didn't go home but to a coffee shop near the hospital. He drank two cups of coffee, postponing the inevitable, but in the end, he couldn't let his friend die alone.

He drove as close as he could get to Anderson Cove then walked through the brush and weeds until he stood near the rotting remains of the pilings that had once supported the vanished docks. A salvage ship with a large crane was loading pieces of the *Harold* onto open barges. Workers milled on the deck, and smoke rose over the brilliant flares and sparks of cutting torches. Little by little, the workers worried at the superstructure, and by nightfall, it and half the main deck were gone. The next morning, the *Harold L* would be stripped to the ribs, and then even they would be loaded onto the waiting barges.

Barely noticing his exhaustion, Winfield left the cove and walked back to his car through the growing dusk.

TERMINAL

THE PASSENGER ARRIVED IN TERMINAL A. He already had a ticket, so he went directly to the waiting area and took a seat. He had been warned that it would be a long wait, and with nothing else to do, he began observing the other passengers. Although some of them seemed purposeful, others were aimless. Most sat in their chairs, shifting uncomfortably, glancing at their watches, and checking their tickets. Occasionally, someone got up to buy something to eat from a vendor or to grab a drink in the terminal lounge. Eventually, everybody visited the rest room. The atmosphere was tense, close, and awkward.

The passenger found himself checking his watch as he shifted uncomfortably in his chair.

"What is taking so long?" he wondered aloud. "I want to be where I'm going."

More time passed. So much time that it seemed time must be running out. To see if he could catch it, the passenger looked again at his watch. Yes, more time had passed, but the watch was still working, so time must not have run out yet. But the passenger had been here for so long now that the name of his destination has grown as hazy as the reasons for his journey.

"Why am I here?" he wondered. "Where am I going?"

The only thing that might tell him was his ticket. He looked at it, and in the departure box, it read, "Terminal A." In the time of departure box was the word, "None." "None," also was in the destination box. "That can't be right," he muttered. "I've been given the wrong ticket."

He went to the ticket counter. "My ticket has no departure and no destination," he told the woman at the counter, offering his ticket.

She looked at it.

"That is correct, sir."

But I want to leave. I have some place to go. Can I change my ticket?"

"There will be a penalty, sir."

"Okay."

"Where would you like to go?"

"Somewhere besides here."

"And when?"

"As soon as possible."

"Certainly, sir. Here you are." She handed him a new ticket. "Go down the escalator and take the shuttle train to Terminal B."

He did, and when he arrived at the end of the line, he went up the escalator to Terminal B and took a seat. All around him, the other passengers seemed uncomfortable and restless. After a time, he checked his ticket.

"Terminal B," he read aloud. "Departure: None. Destination: Unknown."

"I'm obviously going nowhere," he said to himself. "There's no point in staying here."

He went to look for an exit, but all he could find were one-way entrances, all crowded with influx, blocked by turnstiles, and guarded by security personnel with stern faces. A security alert light flashed a perpetual orange. Security announcements played subtly over the PA, warning passengers not to go the wrong way.

The passenger saw some stairs leading to an observation deck, but the curtains were drawn over the window, and a "Closed" sign blocked the bottom of the stairs. There were no observations today.

He went back to the waiting area and sat. After a time, he went to buy something to eat from a vendor, then he had a drink in the terminal lounge. After that, he had to go to the rest room. When he returned to the waiting area, he sat uncomfortably, checked his watch, and once again read his ticket to nowhere.

THE TANK

ON THE FRONT PORCH OF a small frame house, illuminated by a single, bare bulb, stood three young men.

"Come on, Barry. You can't just sit around on graduation night all by yourself."

"What do you have in mind?"

Rob grinned and inclined his dark-haired head toward the third man.

"Cliff and I thought we'd drive out to the school to visit the tank."

"The tank? Haven't you spent enough time in that thing?"

"Just a goodbye visit," Rob insisted. "One last look at Wilson's Vat."

The mention of Al Wilson, the head of the diving school, brought a cross between a smile and a grimace to Barry's face. To give the man credit, Wilson knew his stuff where diving was concerned. But that didn't stop him from being a bastard.

"Yeah," he said musingly. "Wouldn't you love to see the look on the old fart's face if he knew we were *playing* around in his precious training tank?"

"That's what gave us the idea," Cliff said. "We ran into Marc and Andy about an hour ago. Half looped, as usual." He chuckled. "Marc was joking about sneaking in and writing some nasty but all-too-true comments about Wilson on the inside walls of the Vat."

"Marc and Andy are with you? They sure are quiet."

"Out in the truck." Rob pointed. "Their mouths are occupied. Drinking beer."

Andy must have seen the gesture, for he yelled out from Cliff's Blazer.

"Get a move on, Barry!"

Barry peered past the glare of the porch light and dimly made out Andy and Marc's shadowy figures in the back seat.

"You really going to mark up the inside of the tank?" he asked, turning back to Rob and Cliff.

"I doubt it," Rob shrugged. "I just want to get one more look at the place without Wilson screaming at me to quit fuckin' around. We had a few good times there."

"Yeah," Cliff agreed.

"If you guys want to write graffiti," Rob said, "that's okay by me. I won't tell."

Barry shrugged. "Okay. I'll skip the graffiti, but one last visit would be good."

"That's the spirit!" Rob slapped him on the back. Barry locked the front door, and the three of them went out to the Blazer. Rob got in the front passenger seat, and Barry slid in the back next to Marc.

"Hey, Barry boy!" Andy slurred out jocularly, leaning over Marc and taking Barry's shoulder in a watery grip. "Glad you decided to make it. What took you guys so long? You didn't have to twist Barry boy's arm, did you?" He sank back into his seat as Cliff accelerated away from the curb.

"Naw," Marc said, a little less fuzzily than Andy. "But they had to pull his leg!" He and Andy broke up at this then took swigs of their beers.

"Hey, have a brew." Andy reached over the back seat, pulled a cold can out of a large metal-clad ice chest full of beer and ice, and pressed it into Barry's hand.

"Thanks," Barry said as he popped the top.

"I'll have one of those," Rob reached back.

"Me, too," said Cliff.

Andy handed over beers, and a few moments of silence followed as everyone drank.

"These two guys," Marc gestured to Rob and Cliff, "tell you what we're gonna do? I had a fantastic idea. Fantastic. We're gonna tell old Wilson what we think of him all over the insides of his tank. Show him, Andy."

Andy pulled a handful of white grease pencils from his shirt pocket.

"These should do the trick," he said. "What are you going to tell the old bastard?"

"I haven't thought about it," Barry said. "Probably nothing. I don't much care about Wilson, anymore."

"Well, I care," Andy said, then he burped loudly. Marc giggled, but Andy went on without noticing. "You know what I'm going to tell that old sum bitch?"

Barry shook his head, but he needn't have bothered as Andy proceeded with a lengthy diatribe against the head of the diving school. Barry had heard it all before in less inebriated form, so while Andy went on, he only half listened and watched the city fade into the suburbs.

The year at the diving school had been a good one in many ways, despite Wilson, or maybe because of him. Almost immediately after enrolling, Barry met Cliff, and they were soon joined by Rob in a friendship that went beyond the classroom. That friendship, especially with Rob, was what saved Barry when the freeway wreck took Carla and, with her, all his dreams and plans and hopes. When Barry hadn't shown up at the school for several days after the ac-

71

cident, Rob sought him out and learned of the tragedy. But Rob's obviously genuine sympathy was offset by the steady pressure he put on Barry to return to the school. Though Barry often thought Rob put him up to it, even Cliff, normally not inclined to commitment, urged the same. Through the weeks of heavy despair that followed the accident, the two of them kept him going when he would have turned away.

Barry now realized that Rob had done the best thing he could have for him. Instead of harping on the bleakness within his friend or urging him to forget the past, Rob pushed Barry into work, into avenues that led away from the past without denying it. When Barry's mood edged into the sucking mire of depression, Rob engineered incidents calculated to drag him out, forcibly if necessary. Inevitably, one of these incidents brought them under the scrutiny of Al Wilson.

Barry smiled to himself, remembering the stunt in question. It concerned Terry Cole, one of the junior instructors. Terry was likable enough most of the time, and he was a crackerjack welder, but he had a scathing way of criticizing the novice divers, probably because he was, himself, relatively new at the game and insecure about his position at the school. After Barry inadvertently failed to clean some equipment one afternoon, Terry singled him out in front of the entire class as the object of a lecture on incompetence. As Barry fought off the embarrassment and guilt added to his already burdened emotions, Rob hatched a plot for revenge.

The plot came to fruition one afternoon when Barry and Cliff were working in the tank with Terry. They'd been welding a superstructure similar to that of an oil rig, and toward the end of their stint underwater, the two of them maneuvered Terry into a certain, preplanned position. Cliff gave a tug on his signal line, and Rob, who was above, tending his lines, loosened the winch holding the partial super-structure suspended in the water. The superstructure came down to the bottom of the tank, pinning Terry's air hose to the floor without cutting off his air supply.

Furious, Terry struggled to work the air hose free, mouthing obscenities behind his faceplate. With a wave, Barry and Cliff floated upwards. As Barry broke the sur-face, he saw Rob splash the contents of a small bottle around the intake valve of Terry's air compressor. Barry and Cliff grinned at each other as they removed their masks. Marc and Andy were the other two tenders, and they dropped the lines and broke up laughing, gripping their noses. The bottle held a cheap cologne that was used in quantity by Terry's girlfriend, who often traipsed through the corridors of the school, looking for her beau. Within moments, a huge bubble of air burst to the surface, and seconds later, Terry followed, sputtering. He'd left his mask on the bottom, and a trail of tangy bubbles streaked to the surface after him.

The brunt of the matter was that the compressor, hose, and mask were gaggingly pungent for weeks, and whenever any one of the five of them was on a training dive, Terry made them use the tainted equipment. But Terry had been easy on them compared to Wilson. The points the diving chief listed were all reasonable: Any of the three in the water could have been seriously injured or killed by the loosened superstructure, Terry could have drowned if his air supply had been choked off and his body trapped, the tank itself could have been damaged, the superstructure was damaged, and the air compressor, hose, and mask were polluted.

Wilson was of a mind to kick them all out of the school, but Terry interceded. Oddly enough, he hadn't really been angered by the incident and referred to it as the best joke he'd seen in years, even if he'd been the butt of it. Wilson didn't agree, but he was swayed to clemency. Thereafter, Terry loosened up considerably, and Barry found he could learn more from him than from most of the other instructors.

They got off with reprimands—and the provision that they behave themselves in the future. They agreed, but the matter hadn't stopped there, at least as far as Wilson was concerned. He kept close watch of their collective activities, and when he was in a critical mood, which was often, they were his first targets and the last to receive praise. He pushed on them the most difficult jobs, and even detailed them to clean the tank—an unpleasant task involving muriatic acid and chlorine—for an unprecedented three months in a row during the dead of winter. As the year progressed, his punishments relaxed, though his censure did not.

Wilson's watchful eye bound the three of them together even more, and included Marc and Andy in the group. Perhaps it had been Wilson's statements that someone could have been hurt or killed that started them talking about the idea of living with death. But when Barry thought about it, he realized it was just as likely that Rob fastened on the idea in order to sublimate in an intellectual guise Barry's emotional turmoil on the subject. And no doubt their new occupation as divers—an occupation replete with hazards to life and limb—played its own role.

The question—the Great Question—was whether or not one lived more fully when in imminent danger of losing one's life. Did living on the edge make life more intense, meaningful, and enjoyable? For months they kicked around ideas on the subject, but in the end were unable to come to any firm conclusions. They hadn't the experience. All five were in their early twenties, and aside from the minor hellraising usual to teenagers, none of them had been in a situation that could give a basis for an answer. Perhaps it was for that very reason that they were anxious for an answer. As usual, Rob led the debate with his admittedly romantic notions about the natural high experience by men in combat, the adrenaline surges of people engaged in dangerous sports, and the tight-knit camaraderie felt by those employed in dangerous occupations.

Barry often took the opposite standpoint, though, in truth, he wasn't really sure of it. While he felt life was at its best when it contained a degree of uncertainty, he also recognized the need for stability, for some basis from which to approach life. The latter had partly been what Carla had meant to him, and he understood that his own interest in the Great Question was very much a product of his own indecisiveness on the matter since the accident had undercut that stability and thrust him almost totally into the realm of uncertainty.

Of the others, Cliff was most interested in the question. Without taking sides, he followed the arguments and acted as an informal barometer of the persuasiveness of the opposing viewpoints. Marc and Andy listened and occasionally put in their two cents, but neither was sufficiently reflective to maintain an interest.

"Ready for another?" Rob asked over his shoulder.

Barry shook his can, felt a few swallows' worth swish around inside, and shook his head.

"I'm fine."

"What you thinking about?"

"The Great Question."

"Not that shit again," Andy complained. "Why don't you guys get off that kick and talk about something important, like pussy?"

"What would you know about that?" Marc asked, bumping Andy's arm, causing him to slop beer onto his thigh.

"Hey! Watch that, boy!" Andy's voice went up a notch, but a moment later he burst out laughing. "Say, did I tell you guys about that hot brunette...?"

"Only about fifty times," Cliff said, glancing in the rearview mirror.

"You sure I told you? Her name was Marsha. I told you about Marsha?"

"Sure you did," Rob said. "And Annie and Tamma and...."

"I get the picture," Andy sulked.

"Pipe down, you guys," Cliff said. "We're almost there."

"Why we gotta be quiet?" Marc wanted to know. "You know there ain't no guards."

"We're going to be breaking and entering," Rob said decisively, "so let's not do anything stupid to attract attention. Okay?"

"All right," Marc nodded, and the rest of them agreed.

Cliff wheeled the Blazer into the parking lot in front of the school and pulled into a shadowed corner. They all piled out, and Andy and Marc opened the cargo hatch and dragged out the ice chest.

"What the hell you bringing that thing for?" Cliff asked.

"To drink, that's what the hell," Marc answered, and he and Andy laughingly staggered toward the fence, the ice chest suspended between them.

"I hope they don't expect me to help them get that thing over the fence," Cliff said.

"They will if you expect to drink one," Rob said. "But once it's over, we'll let them lug it the rest of the way."

"All right," Cliff grinned. "Let's go help before they dump it all over the place."

They hurried after their inebriated companions, reaching the fence at about the same time.

"Shit, this thing is heavy," Marc complained as they hefted the chest up and over the fence. But after a minute of groaning and cursing, the five of them and the ice chest were safely over the barrier, heading for the tank, which stood illuminated in the light of the waxing moon.

The tank was a simple enough structure—an open-topped cylinder twenty feet in diameter and a little over fifty feet tall. Made of galvanized steel plates flanged and bolted together in 5' x 8' sections, it held nearly 12,000 gallons of water. In it, novice divers practiced actual underwater construction techniques under controlled conditions. Three divers, usually two students and an instructor, worked in the tank at a time, putting together a mock oil rig or bridge stanchion.

For Barry, one of the most interesting aspects of the tank had nothing to do with its function. He had learned early in his schooling that the tank was a giant, if extremely weak, battery. Because of the dissimilarity between the metals of the tank walls and the mock oil rig or bridge stanchion suspended inside, oxidation tended to rob electrons from the tank walls. Left unchecked for long enough, this electrolysis would gradually eat away at the metal plating, causing the tank walls to become dangerously thin. The solution was to place several blocks of zinc, referred to as sacrificial anodes, into the tank. A high oxidizer, the zinc released its electrons to the metal of the oil rig more readily than would the tank walls, so the anodes disintegrated instead of the tank.

Barry followed the others up the steps spiraling to the mouth of the tank. At the top, the steps ended in a landing that forked into two railless catwalks that traversed the mouth of the tank. The two grilled walkways paralleled each other at a distance of five feet. From them, divers descended and the tenders played out air and safety lines.

Walking out onto one of the catwalks, Barry stared at the surface of the dark water, oily looking in the moonlight. He bit his lip as thoughts of Carla flooded through his mind, unbidden but implacable. She'd loved the look of moonlight on water. There was a bitter taste in his mouth. The schooling and discipline had been good for him, but without her....

Marc and Andy staggered onto the other catwalk and dropped the ice chest with a metallic bang.

"Quiet!" Cliff hissed, and Marc and Andy giggled drunkenly, poking each other.

"I can't see nothing. Maybe we should turn on the lights," Andy said, sending him and Marc deeper into mirth. He was referring to the two large arc lamps poised over the mouth of the tank, used to illuminate the water for night classes. Barry wished he could illuminate the well of anguish within himself as easily. But his sorrow was deeper than the water of the tank, and he couldn't seem to find a light to brighten it.

"Something on your mind, buddy?" Rob was suddenly next to him on the catwalk. He had a beer in each hand and gave one to Barry.

"Same old shit," Barry said, popping the tab and taking a drink. He stared reflectively at the dark, still surface just below him.

"A great day," he said sarcastically, lifting his beer in a mock salute. "To the future." He took another swallow.

"I know you wish she was here," Rob told him. "You two had a great thing together. But she's not...."

"I can sure see that," Barry hissed. Rob held up his hand.

"Words of truth, my friend, not meant to injure."

"Okay," Barry acknowledged. "Sorry. It's just that it was so...." He shook his head and sighed.

"We all wish we could have it so good," Rob said gently. "But sooner or later, you'll just have to let it go."

"Yeah, Barry, let it go," Andy said too loudly from the other catwalk.

"Shut up." Cliff shoved Andy, who turned and shoved back.

78

"Shut up, yourself, jerk," Andy said without rancor. "If Barry can't take a little needling from a buddy, he might as well jump off right now." He gestured over the side of the tank.

"All I meant was for you to leave him alone so he could get to the bottom of what's bugging him," Cliff said.

"We all know what's bugging Barry," Marc put in.

"Well, Marc," Rob said levelly. "Since you know so much, why don't you tell us your opinion?"

"Shit," Marc hedged. "We all know it's that Carla chick...."

"Look," Barry said. "Let's just forget the whole thing, okay?"

"We can all forget it fine," Andy said. "It's you who can't."

"Why the hell should I forget?" Barry demanded harshly. "Why the hell? Would you?"

"I'd sure as hell...."

"You'd sure as hell be sobbing in your beer right now," Rob interrupted. "Now, let's knock it off. We didn't come up here to discuss Barry's tragedy. We came up here to celebrated our graduation from this tank to the oceans of the world."

"You sound like a politician," Marc laughed, and the rest of them joined in, the strain broken. Cliff sat on the catwalk, removed his shoes, and dangled his bare feet over the edge, splashing them in the water. Rob nudged Barry, motioning for him to walk to the far end of the catwalk, away from the others. Shrugging, Barry complied, though he didn't really feel like talking about anything at the moment.

"What do you think you'll do now that school's over?" Rob asked as they reached the end of the catwalk, where it was joined to the other by a platform. Barry shrugged.

"Don't know for sure. I guess I'll try to get a job diving. That's what I spent the last year here for."

"You planning on staying in the area?"

"I suppose. Why?"

"Cliff and I are thinking of heading down the coast. Lots of oil rig work, and they're putting in that new navy base."

"I'd have to think about it. I don't know. Things have changed so much since the accident. I'm not really sure just what I want."

"Keep it in mind. We'll probably hang around here for another month or so, taking the summer easy. Then we'll head out. Plenty of time to decide."

"I'll remember."

"Well," Rob said, shaking his now empty can. "Ready for another?"

"Not yet," Barry replied. "Still got half."

"I think I'll get one." Rob stepped onto the catwalk that held their friends and walked toward them. Barry followed.

A friendly argument was in progress when the two of them reached the ice chest. Cliff and Andy were at each other again, this time over the most appropriate method of leaving graffiti on the inside of the tank walls.

"If we go down and get a scuba rig, we can get right to the bottom." Andy swayingly gestured over the side of the tank, toward the low building where the diving gear was kept.

"That's right," Cliff countered. "And I guess you'll be the one who breaks down the door to get at the scuba gear?"

"Shit," Andy grimaced. He reached into his back pocket and pulled out his wallet, nearly dropping it into the water as he fumbled it open. "I got a goddamn credit card in here somewhere. Can't use it to buy nothing, but we can just stick it between the door and the lock, and it'll pop right open."

"You've been watching too many movies," Rob said genially. "Or too many TV commercials. American Express can't get you in everywhere. That lock's all wrong for a credit card."

"Well, what are you going to do?" Andy asked belligerently, chin stuck out.

"I'm not going to do anything," Rob stated. "Except keep your drunken ass out of trouble."

"I don' need no help with my drunken ass," Andy groused, but he jammed the wallet back into his pocket anyway.

"We can free dive down to write something," Marc ventured.

"What I got to say to Wilson would take all night to write if I keep having to come up for air," Andy sulked. "Besides, I wanted to write it down at the bottom. You know that's too far for me to free dive. I really gotta get some gear."

"You're too drunk to dive," Cliff commented.

"And you're not drunk enough," Andy said, opening the ice chest and extracting two beers. He tossed one to Cliff and opened the other for himself. "If I can't have no gear, then I'll have me a beer." He burst into laughter, and the rest of them followed. During the next few minutes, the momentary tension was forgotten as the five of them enjoyed their beers in the cool of the night.

Barry felt much better than he had a few minutes before. The beers set up a warm glow enhanced by his friends' bantering, and the clear sky and light breeze gave no companionship to his troubled emotions. He realized that the sorrow and grief of the past months was going to lift. Life would feel like more than just existence.

His reverie was broken by a sudden intensifying of sound behind him. Another argument had broken out, this time between Marc and Cliff. Their voices suddenly rose to a loud pitch, and a scuffle ensued. Barry was just in the act of turning, when a body struck him from behind, almost sending him to his knees. Rob had fallen against him, and as they both regained their balance, the scuffling ended abruptly with a thump and a heavy splash.

Barry turned to see Cliff standing over Marc, who was sitting dazedly on the catwalk.

"You bastard," Cliff grated out. "Don't ever say that to me again."

"Big man...," Marc began, but ceased when Cliff took a menacing step forward.

"Cool it, you guys," Rob ordered. "This is supposed to be a celebration, remember?"

"What fell into the water?" Barry asked abruptly. The others turned to stare at him in the dim light.

"I don't know," Marc said, getting to his feet. "When this jerk pushed me, I bumped into something...."

"Where's Andy?" Barry asked. The others stared dumbly at him. Taking two strides, he was at the edge of the catwalk just behind Marc. The surface was broken by a thin stream of bubbles streaking up from the depths. "Shit! Did you knock Andy into the water?" He grabbed Marc's shoulders in an awkward sideways grip and shook them. Marc twisted out of his grasp.

"How the hell should I know?"

"Well, where the hell is he?"

"If he fell in the water, he can swim. Why worry?"

"You see him swimming?"

Suddenly all four of them were at the edge, staring at the bubbles trailing to the surface.

"Maybe he hit his head or something," Cliff ventured.

"He's pretty plastered."

"What are we going to do?" Marc asked, suddenly more sober than he'd been moments before.

Barry jerked off his shoes and wriggled out of his jeans and t-shirt. He looked at Marc.

"Go down and turn on the arc lights," he said. Without another word, he took several deep breaths and dove into the black water.

He swam downward through the dark effervescence of his dive. Within seconds, he located the trail of bubbles rising from the depths of the tank, and almost as if climbing hand-over-hand along the trail, he groped downward. The water around him darkened as he descended, and it was all he could do to see the thin stream of bubbles as they rose toward him. The pressure began to build steadily on him, and he had to swallow to equalize the stress on his eardrums.

He wondered if he had enough air for the dive. He'd been hasty in diving into the tank, and truthfully, he doubted his ability to bring an unconscious person to the surface all the way from the bottom. But he had little choice. He was already a third of the way down, and Andy had to be pulled from the water soon or he'd drown. A deep-seated panic gripped his heart as he saw an image of his friend being hauled out of the tank by block and tackle, dead, bloated, accusing with blank, bulging eyes.

The water around him seemed to get thicker as he groped deeper, the silvery nodes of rising bubbles visible only when they were within an inch of his face. He kept one arm extended, feeling his way, dreading contact with his friend's body almost as much as he dreaded not finding him. Terrible stories from older divers who had participated in underwater searches for drowning victims flashed through his brain with vivid clarity. Any moment he would feel the hair of the dead man twine around his fingers with a siren's grip, pull him deeper and deeper until....

He nearly gasped out in panic, but instead, he steeled his heaving heart and pulled his senses inward, away from the growing pressure around him. He now felt as much as saw the trail of bubbles as they reached him. They were thinning out. His friend must be nearly out of air, lungs full of water. Barry had to reach him soon, whatever the cost.

"Where are you, Andy?" a strangely calm part of Barry's mind called out, but it seemed a tiny voice in this black, pressure-filled eternity. His lungs were leaden, and hot flashes sparked through his brain as his tissues screamed for relief. But though his legs and arms were growing stiff, he forced himself deeper.

Suddenly the trail of bubbles ran out, leaving him in directionless darkness, crushed, aching, lungs straining.

He paused momentarily, orienting himself through flailing senses. When he had down fixed in his mind, he clawed himself in that direction, wondering if he'd be able to find his friend in all that darkness before he was forced to surface. Then, suddenly, shockingly in this liquid world of black, senseless pressure, his outstretched hand struck the metal floor of the tank.

Reaching the bottom was so stunning that he almost reacted automatically and just pushed off toward the surface. But his friend's need restrained him, and as deliberately as he could, he groped along the invisible plating, arms stretched wide. Within seconds, his left arm struck a hard, angular object.

"Sacrificial anode." His mind automatically made the identification, and he pulled away, continuing his search. A moment later, he encountered another anode. His movements were becoming sluggish, and he could barely do more than just float there in the water. His consciousness seemed to be narrowing down to a tunnel of almost intolerable brightness. Then blindingly, the brightness was all around him, flooding the formerly dark water with brilliant illumination.

Dazed, he looked around. Marc had gotten to the arc lamps and turned them on. Quickly he scanned the circumference of the tank bottom, looking for Andy. He saw several anodes, but of his friend there was no sign. Shocked, he scanned the bottom again, his eyes stopping on one of the anodes. It was larger than the rest, and had a curious look to it. With the last strokes he was capable of, he moved over to it, seeing with dull surprise that it was not an anode but the metal ice chest. A couple of bubbles of air oozed around the edge of the lid and bounded toward the distant surface.

With effort, Barry pushed off the bottom and followed, stroking weakly, depleted air bursting from his lungs. Gasping, he broke the surface, flailed for the catwalk, and missed. There was a splash next to him, and strong arms shoved him forward, into the catwalk. He grabbed hold as another pair of arms reached down and held him firmly. He looked up to see Cliff standing over him. From beside him in the water, Rob's voice came urgently.

"Where is he?"

"Not there," Barry gasped.

"Not there?" Cliff almost shouted. "What do you mean?"

"He's not down there." Barry took a deep gulp. "It was the ice chest."

"The ice chest!" Rob roared, sounding angry and relieved at the same time.

"That's all," Barry said.

"Where the fuck is he?" Cliff grated.

Rob grunted his puzzlement, but Barry, too tired to care, merely clung to the wet metal grating. At that moment there came a dull, metallic bang that reverberated through the structure of the tank, followed by a distant whooshing sound. Almost immediately, the water level in the tank began to drop drastically.

"The dump valve!" Cliff shouted. "Marc popped the dump valve!" He ran to the edge of the tank and looked over.

The dump valve was designed to quickly empty the tank in an emergency. By the time Cliff reached the edge, the water had receded below Barry and Rob's feet, leaving them dangling from the catwalk. Barry had his arms up on the metal grid, supporting his body, while Rob, also stripped to his underwear, was left hanging by his hands from one of the struts just below the walkway.

"What the hell you do that for?" Cliff yelled over the side of the tank.

"He must have thought Andy was still at the bottom," Rob said, then he worked his way hand over hand to a position next to Barry. "You okay, buddy?" he asked.

"Yeah," Barry said, looking down at the receding water, now thirty feet below. In a matter of moments, virtually all the water would be gone, leaving him and Rob above a fifty-foot fall to the metal floor. Light from the arc lamps glinted off the curvature of the wet metal walls. Rob was still hanging by his hands, and he started to swing back and forth, chuckling.

"Look!" he called out. "Like Tarzan. I haven't done this since I was a kid."

"Careful," Barry warned, lifting his head from the catwalk. "It's slippery."

"Careful!" Rob shouted, a broad grin slicing across his face. "Sounds like you might be afraid of falling." He slowed his swing, coming to a stop. Shifting his grip, he said, "What about the Great Question, partner? I though you were always in favor of testing theories. We got a perfect opportunity right here."

"What do you mean?"

"Well, check our position, my friend. Kind of high-and-dry, you might say. Now check out that other catwalk." With his chin, Rob indicated the other walkway five feet from them. "Suppose you and I just swing right over there?"

"From here?"

"Of course from here. Where else are you?"

Barry felt his still-labored breathing and the quivering in his arms, and he shook his head.

"I'm not sure I'm up to it."

"Come on, Barry. Where's your sense of adventure? We have the answer to the Great Question right here. Are you afraid to find it out?"

"I'm not afraid," Barry said. "It just seems pointless."

Rob laughed and swung his body into a shallow arc. "Rationalizations," he snorted.

By this time, the tank was practically empty, with perhaps a foot of water remaining at the bottom. Barry could hear the soft clang of feet climbing the steps to the top of the tank and realized that Marc was coming back. He hoped Marc would get there in time to talk some sense into Rob. He could tell he wasn't going to be able to, and Cliff was betraying excitement at Rob's suggestion. Here was Cliff's chance to know, vicariously as usual. If he could only delay Rob a few moments....

"Look, Rob," he began. "There's nothing to prove. It's not a matter of courage, it's more...."

"Talk all you want, buddy," Rob spat out. "Here's the answer to what I want to know, so look out, and stay back. Cliff, will you help this guy back to safety?"

Barry blanched at the vehement sarcasm in Rob's voice as Cliff bent down and got a firm grip on his arms.

By this time, Rob was swinging smoothly over the yawning pit, his attention focused on the other catwalk. Barry became aware that Marc had just reached the top of the tank when Rob let go with a whoop. His body arced across the space between the catwalks, arms reaching, hands grasping for the struts on the far side. His left hand struck against the struts first, and bounced off. For a sickening instant, Barry envisioned his friend plunging into the lighted pit of the tank, but Rob's right hand caught the strut, slipped, then held. His breath was coming hard and fast, and by the way he gingerly reached up to grasp the strut with his left hand, Barry knew he was hurt.

"Get him!" Cliff shot over his shoulder at Marc, who was staring dumbfounded at Rob's form dangling over the pit from one catwalk and Barry from the other. "Hurry!"

As Cliff began to haul Barry onto the walkway, Marc dashed over to Rob and hauled him to safety. A moment later, Andy's head rose over the edge of the tank.

"What the fuck is going on?" he demanded with drunken petulance.

"Where the fuck were you?" Cliff finished pulling Barry to safety then turned on Andy.

"What do you mean where the fuck was I?" Andy turned belligerent.

"The stupid son of a bitch was down there trying to break into the scuba equipment shack," Marc answered as he gave the final tug that brought Rob onto the catwalk. "He came up to me just after I dumped the tank."

"We thought you were drowned," Barry said, standing slowly. "It was just the ice chest, though."

"The ice chest?" Andy looked puzzled. "What happened to the ice chest?"

Wordlessly, Barry pointed into the tank. Andy looked down, saw the chest, and began cursing about lost beer.

"Shut up," Rob grated. "You don't even know what good friends you have."

Andy looked up and began to retort, but Cliff stopped him.

"Shut up," Cliff said.

"Yeah," Barry agreed. "Shut up."

Andy's mouth snapped closed, and he glared at them but said nothing else. Marc looked on with an uncomprehending stare.

"We'd better get outta here," Cliff said, and Barry nodded agreement as he stepped into his jeans.

"What about the ice chest?" Marc asked.

"You want it, you go down and get it," Rob said, voice tired. He finished buckling his belt then bent for his shoes. After putting them on, he walked to the end of the catwalk, nursing his arm, and stepped onto the landing to the stairs that led to the ground. A moment later, the rest of them followed, Marc and Andy looking disgruntled.

"You guys go on," Rob said when they all reached the bottom. "I want to talk to Barry for a minute."

Puzzled, Barry stayed behind while the others splashed through the remains of 12,000 gallons of water soaking the ground around the tank and pooling in the adjacent parking lot. When they reached the fence, Rob spoke.

"I'm sorry I needled you up there," he began, and Barry tried to say it was all right, but Rob held up his good hand.

"You know, while I was swinging up there, I thought you were the most cowardly fool in the world. I mean, we had the answer to the Great Question right in our hands, and you were too chicken to find out the answer. But after I let go, it was different. I saw that slippery catwalk, felt myself hurtle toward it, and realized I was the cowardly fool, taking unnecessary risks to salvage my pride. I think I was hurt that you took the initiative and risk by diving for Andy. Maybe I had to prove something to myself or Cliff. I don't know. But I think I do know part of the reason you didn't jump with me. I know you were exhausted from the dive, but that wasn't really it. If there had been a reason, you would have jumped. But there wasn't. You were right—it was pointless. I didn't believe you until it was too late and I was in flight, but I understand now. You risked everything to save Andy, and that had a point to it, but to risk for the sake of the risk is foolish."

"It wasn't all that complicated when I did it," Barry assured him. "I just thought Andy was in the water, so I went to help. But maybe what we did wasn't so different. When the lights came on and I found myself at the bottom, out of air and alone, I felt like an idiot risking my life for an ice chest." They both laughed. "Anyway, I'm glad we were together when we got the answers we were looking for."

"Maybe we all have to learn the hard way," Rob sighed.

"How's the arm?" Barry asked.

"Hurts, but I don't think it's busted," Rob replied, nursing it with the other hand. "It'll be okay." He turned to go to the Blazer, but Barry stopped him.

"Hey," Barry said. "I think I'll go down the coast with you guys."

"That's great," Rob said, and the two of them sloshed to the fence. After climbing over, Barry turned for one last look at the tank. They'd forgotten to turn off the blazing arc lamps, and glittering light splashed over the soaked ground.

"I guess that mess is as good as graffiti," he commented, and the two of them were still chuckling as they climbed into Cliff 's truck.

ABOUT FACE

"Who's the new guy?"

"New guy?"

"Yeah. That guy over there in the charcoal suit. Talking to Margie."

"You mean Bill?"

"Bill?"

"Bill Thompson." Jim gave him a funny look.

"Come on," Rick said. "Who is he?"

Jim glanced at the man and woman then back at Rick.

"I just see Bill and Margie."

"Okay," Rick said. "If it's some kind of secret, and you don't want to tell me...."

Jim peered around, looked back at Rick, and gave a nervous chuckle.

"I don't see anybody else, Rick."

"If that's Bill, what happened to him? Did he have some kind of plastic surgery?"

"Nothing happened to him." Jim squinted at him. "You feeling okay?"

Rick, suddenly afraid, gave an unsteady grin and said, "Just messing with you, Jim."

"Well," Jim said with another nervous chuckle. "You sure had me going."

"Yeah," Rick said. "I guess I better get back to work." He turned and went into his office.

He'd known Bill Thompson, the department supervisor, for seven years, and the man talking to Margie, who was Bill's personal assistant, definitely wasn't Bill Thompson.

But why had Jim insisted it was? Was he some kind of honcho from Corporate? An auditor, maybe? If so, it wouldn't be any skin off Rick's nose to know. He was just a paper pusher and didn't have any control over anything financial.

He'd have to check with Bill Thompson—the real Bill Thompson. He'd tell him.

Rick waited half an hour so if Jim saw him going into Bill's office, he wouldn't think anything of it. As he approached Bill's office, he saw Margie emerge, carrying a couple of manila file folders.

"Is Bill in his office?"

"Yeah. Go on in." She went off down the hall.

Rick watched her go, then he rapped on Bill's door and went in.

The stranger in the charcoal suit was sitting at Bill's desk.

He was the only person there. He looked up as Rick came into the room, a questioning look in his eyes.

"Something I can do for you, Rick?"

Funny, but he actually did sound a little like Bill.

"Uh, no, uh." Rick backed out of the room. "Sorry. I was just looking for Margie."

The questioning look in the man's eyes grew slightly more puzzled, but then he disappeared around the door frame as Rick hurried back to his own office.

Once there, Rick sat for a few minutes, wondering what was going on. It had to be something unusual for both Jim and Margie to claim that the stranger was Bill. But at least he could verify that something was happening, even if no one would say what. He emerged from his office and went to the reception area.

"Hi, Patricia," he said to the receptionist. "Have you seen a stranger walking around the office this morning? He's about Bill Thompson's height and weight, with brown hair, and he's wearing a charcoal-colored suit."

Patricia frowned. "No, I don't think so. We haven't had any visitors this morning that I know of."

"Okay," he said. "Well, let me know if you see anybody, will you?"

"All right," she replied, giving him a curious stare.

Rick went to Annie's door.

"Say, have you noticed anybody visiting the office today who isn't normally here?"

"No," she said, looking up from her desk. "Not unless you count the Fed Ex man."

"Do me a favor, will you? Walk by Bill's office and look in there, then come back and tell me who's in there with him. But don't say anything to them, okay?"

"Are you serious?"

"Come on." He gave a quick smile. "Just make it natural."

"All right," she said. "I have to make some copies, any-how." She got up, her plump breasts jiggling, and picked up several sheets off her desk.

Rick watched her go down the hall. As she passed Bill's office, she casually glanced in. Then she went to the photo-copier, made copies of the papers in her hand, and came back, again glancing into Bill's office.

"Bill's the only one in there," she said as she edged around Rick and sat in her chair.

"He's alone?"

"Yes." She frowned. "Something wrong?"

"No," he said. "Nothing. There was someone else in there a few minutes ago, and I just wondered who he was."

"Well, Bill's in there by himself, now, and I haven't seen anyone except the usual staff this morning."

"Okay. Thanks."

Rick headed down the hall. He'd kept an eye on the passageway since Annie had come back, and no one had entered or left Bill's office. As he passed by, he gave a quick glance through the doorway.

The stranger was at Bill's desk, talking into the phone while he read something on his computer screen.

Rick hurried back to his own office and sat leadenly in his chair.

Why was everyone lying to him? It couldn't be a practical joke, though it had to be. Whatever it was, Rick didn't find it amusing. He tried to get some work done, but he couldn't concentrate. Grabbing a thick file, he went out to the photocopier and spent half an hour copying the file three times, observing as people came and went. No one seemed to notice that the stranger in Bill's office was anyone other than Bill Thompson. But if it was a practical joke, they'd have seen Rick in the hallway and wouldn't have let on. Rick somehow had to observe the stranger with some of the staff when no one knew he was watching.

After thinking about it for half an hour, he couldn't figure out how he could manage it. But there was something he *could* do. He left the office, took the elevator to the snack shop on the first floor of the building, and went over to the pay phone. He couldn't use the phone in his office because of caller ID, and the same went for his cell phone. The pay phone would make his call anonymous. He dialed the main office number, and when Patricia's voice came on the line, he lowered his voice a couple of registers and asked for Mr. Thompson. Patricia told him to hold, and a few moments later, the stranger's voice came over the receiver.

"This is Bill Thompson. Can I help you?"

The voice, disembodied from the strange face, sounded even more like Bill's than before.

Rick hung up without speaking, hurried back to the elevators, and reentered the office through the back door, as if he'd been gone to the rest room. No one saw him, but he did spot the stranger still sitting at Bill's desk.

Okay, you bastards, Rick thought. I'll catch you. I know what to do. He looked up Bill's name in the company directory, left the office early, and drove to the expensive west Houston subdivision where Bill lived. At first, Rick intended to just go up, ring Bill's doorbell, and confront his supervisor, but the sight of two boys playing catch in the front yard made him stop. He recognized the boys as Bill's children, though he hadn't seen them in six months or so.

Realizing how foolish he'd look at being so taken in by the joke that he'd driven all the way out here, he didn't stop but drove on by. Ten minutes later, he was nearing the intersection that provided egress from the subdivision, and while he waited for the light, he saw the stranger approach the light from the direction of the freeway and turn into the subdivision.

The fact that he was driving Bill's car—or one just like it —was almost as shocking as seeing him here at all.

The stranger hadn't noticed Rick, and Rick quickly backed up and turned around in the middle of the street. A sinking feeling invading his gut, Rick followed the man as he made straight for Bill's house. Rick stopped half a block away, watching the stranger pull into Bill's driveway. When the man emerged from the car, the boys called, "Hey, Dad," and laughed and tossed him the ball. He played catch with them for a couple of minutes then, carrying his briefcase, went to the front door. It opened, and Bill's wife was there. She gave him a kiss and a hug, and they disappeared into the house.

Rick, dumbfounded, drove out of the subdivision, barely seeing where he was going. If the stranger was someone's idea of a practical joke, it had gone way beyond the funny stage. And that whole domestic scene with the kids and wifely affection was just too elaborate and natural not to be real, even if there was an artificial quality about it, sort of like something he'd seen once too often on TV. But the hell of it was that no one could have suspected that Rick would go to Bill's house, so why had the charade continued there? Rick could see the boys pretending the stranger was their dad, but would Bill's wife actually hug and kiss him?

As he neared home, Rick pulled into the parking lot of a bar. Usually, he drank only in moderation and rarely during the week, but he needed something to brace himself. Even more, he needed a quiet place to collect his thoughts before he went home to Betty.

Rick had been in this bar only a few times. In the quiet and dark, he could see that a couple of the tables were occupied, three people were at the bar, and in the far corner, two men clicked balls across the felt of the sole pool table.

Rick ordered a bourbon and Coke at the bar and carried the drink to an empty table somewhat apart from the occupied ones. He loosened his tie, sipped at his drink, and tried to make sense of the man with Bill's name and office and family but not his face. At first, Rick had assumed that it was some kind of practical joke aimed at him, though he couldn't fathom what its purpose might be. But when the apparent joke continued elsewhere when no one could have suspected Rick might see, he had to revise his thoughts. A joke was only one possibility. The other was that he was becoming delusional.

But didn't they say that if you think you're crazy, you aren't? He knew that was bull. Lots of schizophrenics know they're nuts when they aren't under the influence of their delusions. It seemed like he'd once read that most schizo-phrenics begin exhibiting symptoms as late teens or in their early twenties, but didn't it sometimes strike people later in life? Maybe it was some kind of chemical imbalance. That happened to people. Some gland or other pumping too much or too little, and suddenly you weren't normal any more. It had to be that, or something like it. He wasn't par-ticularly stressed at work, his five-year-old marriage was do-ing fine, and he and Betty were finally in a financial position to seriously talk about having kids.

It had to be chemical. Or, he thought in a sudden rush of fear, maybe it was a brain tumor causing hallucinations. He hadn't had a full physical in a couple of years. He was still young. What could go wrong? Now, though, he reflect-ed, it probably was time to call the doctor and go in. Wasn't that what he paid all those health insurance premiums for?

Yeah, he thought, leaning back and pushing down thoughts of cancer. Seeing Bill as someone else was just some weird effect of a chemical imbalance. He'd just ignore it until he had a physical.

He lifted his glass to take a drink when the two men playing pool caught his attention. The pool table was in a darkened corner, the only light a wedge of brilliance shining down from the florescent fixture suspended over the table. One of the men was bent over the table. He took his shot, missed, and stood, his face and upper torso vanishing in the gloom. The other player, also hidden in the shadows, walked half way around the table, then leaned into the light to line up his shot.

It was the stranger who'd taken Bill's identity.

By the time the shock fully registered on Rick, the man had shot. A ball clunked into a pocket, and the man moved to the other side of the table, his face again obscured.

Rick knew it was not possible that Bill—the stranger—even had he known that Rick had been at his house, could have beaten Rick here. Besides, this had been a random stop, and the man already was playing pool when Rick came in.

Wasn't he?

Rick got up and went over to the pool table as if he merely wanted to watch the game. As he moved, he felt disembodied, as if what was happening wasn't real. The man with the face was lining up another shot. His face was undoubtedly similar to that of the stranger with Bill's name, but there were differences. This man's face was slightly more rugged and weathered, as if he worked outside. His clothes —jeans, a plaid shirt, and western boots—backed up the impression. It was the same face, but not exactly the same.

Pondering chemical imbalances and hallucinations, Rick left the bar and drove home. Best not mention anything to Betty, he thought. Visit the doctor first and see what he has to say, then there'll really be something to tell Betty.

And he could hope that whatever it was that was working on him would go away on its own.

It didn't. Bill retained the stranger's face, though Rick had to admit that, once he started talking to him, he seemed like Bill in every other respect. He certainly seemed to have Bill's memories as well as his knowledge of the job. His voice was even Bill's. If there was anything different, it seemed to be a slight air of formality that hung over the new Bill. Even on casual Fridays, he continued to wear his conservative business suits, though in the past he'd often dressed in slacks and a sports shirt.

But Rick didn't have a chance to grow accustomed to the new Bill before he saw the face again when he went to the dry cleaners on Friday to drop off his clothes. Alma, the short, fat Hispanic woman behind the counter looked up as he came in.

"Hello, Mr. Marks," she said over the tinny Spanish dialog issuing from the faulty little TV at the far end of the counter.

She had the face.

It was feminized and fleshed to match Alma's rotund build, but it was unmistakably the same face. And at the same time, she was unmistakably Alma. Rick recognized her voice, her long, graying, loose hair, and the unusual pattern of color on her fingernails that he'd noticed the last time he was in as much as he did her heavy hips and the way she walked. She even interrupted him while he was counting his items as she usually did, making him have to recount. Rick left without saying anything other than his usual shallow pleasantries, but as he got in his car, he fervently hoped his condition wouldn't worsen before he could see the doctor.

The day of the physical came, and not only did the man in line ahead of him at the reception counter have the face, so did the receptionist who checked him in. If they, or anyone other than Rick, noticed, no one gave a sign.

Thankfully, Dr. Salmon looked his normal self as he poked and prodded and asked questions. Rick said nothing about his mental condition, deciding to wait until the results had come in. If the results were unusual, he'd tell the doctor. If not, well.... He wasn't sure what he'd do.

In the two weeks between the exam and his return visit to get the results, two more people in the office took on the face. Worse, Rick was seeing the face dozens of times a day, everywhere he went. Here it was with a slightly more rugged jaw, there embedded in fat or with hollow cheeks. It was young and old, light, tan, swarthy, dark. It was on tall and short. It was happy, it was sad. Once, he even saw a whole family at a restaurant, all wearing the same face.

And no one seemed to notice.

When he returned to Dr. Salmon for the report, the doctor told him his cholesterol level was slightly elevated and he was packing a few extra pounds, but otherwise, he was in good health. The only thing that was wrong was that Dr. Salmon now had the face, too. Rick left without saying anything.

He didn't go back to work, however. He went straight home. Betty was still at work. In the bathroom, he examined his own face. With relief, he saw that he was still Rick. Still had Rick's face.

He wasn't sure what he was going to do. Go to a psychiatrist? "Doctor, everyone has a different face than they had before, and they're all the same face."

Yeah, he thought. What if the psychiatrist had the face, too, or took it on while Rick was talking about it? How did these people look when their old face changed to the new? It was too scary to contemplate.

Or was it paranoia?

But no, that was where everyone was out to get you. So far, no one with the face seemed to pay the slightest attention to Rick aside from normal everyday dealings. Even odder, none of the people who didn't have the face seemed to notice that the face was proliferating among them. Were all those people like Rick: too shocked to say anything at first and now too afraid?

He decided to try it on Betty. That evening, as they ate, he asked, "Have you noticed anything unusual about people these days? Everyone seems to be dressing the same. They all look alike."

"I hadn't noticed," she said. "Some kind of style?"

"It's more than clothes," he said, not wanting to be too literal. "Maybe it's makeup styled so everyone looks similar."

"I hadn't noticed." She shrugged and changed the subject. "Jack and Gail invited us over on Saturday."

"Okay," he replied distractedly.

On Saturday, Gail had the face.

"There's something different about Gail," Rick whispered to Betty while they were alone for a few minutes. "Did she change her hair or something?"

"I don't think so," Betty said. "She looks the same as ever."

Later, as Jack was showing Rick his new garden shed, Rick asked, "So, how is Gail? She looks different for some reason."

"She does? I don't know. I don't think she's changed anything, and I think I'd've noticed."

About three weeks later, Betty went to the grocery store and came home with the face.

By now, about half the people Rick saw daily had the face, so he wasn't surprised, but he was disturbed nonetheless. He spent the entire evening surreptitiously interrogating this stranger in his house before he came to realize that she was not a stranger but was Betty. Only her face had changed.

No, there were subtle changes that had gone on under the skin, too. A slight rigidity. A slight coolness. She didn't listen to music while she cooked or did her housework, and she stopped puttering around in her modest flower bed, which she always had loved to do on Sunday afternoons. Instead, she just sat in the den and watched TV—mostly sitcoms—and she laughed right along with the laugh track, her voice indistinguishable from the canned ones coming from the speakers.

The following week, Rick asked Bill Thompson for a couple of days off. He told the supervisor he wanted to take his wife for a long weekend to San Antonio. Bill said okay, and Rick went home and told Betty he had to go to San Antonio on business. Rick didn't often have to go out of town, but it wasn't unheard of, and Betty didn't seem to think anything unusual of it.

"I'll have the girls over on Saturday night," she told him, meaning her four closest friends. "We'll do stamping," she finished, meaning their new shared hobby of ornamenting things and making cute invitations and such with decorative rubber stamps they collected. "It's so darling," they'd say, or "How precious." "I just love it," they'd all crow in unison when one of them came up with an innovative way to combine images.

Rick thought that would be perfect since all four of Betty's friends now looked just like Betty. Their only distinguishing features were hair color and style and differences in build, and that was the only way Rick could tell them apart when they were together. He began to take it on faith that it was the real Betty who remained behind after the others left.

But even the few differences between them were vanishing. Of the five of them, Joan had the flattest chest, but lately, it seemed as if her bust had gotten almost as large as Betty's. And the hair styles were mostly just variations on a common theme. As for hair color, well, most of that was out of the bottle, anyway.

On Thursday morning, Rick drove to San Antonio, which was about 180 miles west of Houston along I-10. But he didn't take the interstate. Instead, he drove on U.S. 90, which wound through the countryside south of I-10, passing through numerous small towns. He took it slow. He stopped in this town for coffee, that town for a snack, and the next to use the rest room. At last, he reached San Antonio and checked into a motel. Inside the safety of his room, he practically rushed to the bathroom and stared in the mirror.

"Thank, God," he breathed, seeing good ol' Rick staring back.

Everywhere he'd stopped along his route and in San Antonio itself, nearly everyone had the face. He could only surmise that it was the same everywhere since most of the national newscasters and practically everyone else on TV had the face. He was having a hell of a time telling anyone apart.

That night, he caught a movie on TV he knew had been made before the face began appearing on, it seemed, nearly everyone but him. Nobody in the movie had the face, though he'd recently seen a photograph of one of the stars, and she now had the face.

Rick didn't know what to think or what he was going to do. What could he do? A psychiatrist certainly was now out of the question. What could he say to a therapist? "Everyone has the same face, doctor. Even you."

He thought about running, but where could he run to? And with what? He could conceivably squirrel away a couple of months' salary before the bill collectors started calling, and Betty would be none the wiser until he vanished. But that would be a few thousand at the most, and he knew he wouldn't last long on that. Then what? No job, on the lam.... And from what, exactly? It didn't sound like a promising future.

He checked out of the motel at dawn, and thinking to escape the face, he drove as far west along I-10 as he could before dusk fell, which put him in Van Horn. He checked into a motel, went to a restaurant, and walked around town, and every single person he saw had the face.

When Rick first started seeing the face, the odd thing had been that no one else noticed it appearing on the people they knew. Then, the odd thing was that no one seemed to notice that Rick *didn't* have the face.

The next morning, Rick had to revise his opinion as well as his observation. There was one person he saw in the convenience store gas station where he stopped to fill up before leaving Van Horn who didn't have the face.

He was in his mid twenties, maybe ten years younger than Rick. When Rick entered the store, the young man was at the counter, buying a phone card and an armful of drinks and snacks. The fact that he didn't look up as Rick entered and walked right by him made Rick take note. Not only did he not have the face, there was something furtive about his behavior, and he kept his eyes turned to the stuff he'd piled on the counter, not meeting the clerk's eyes, either.

Rick glanced outside and saw an older dark blue SUV pulled up at the gas pump next to the one where Rick's car was. Rick went back to his car and stood by, pretending to monitor the pump as it filled his tank. After another minute, the young man hurried outside and over to his SUV.

"Hey," Rick called as the young man unlocked the car and tossed his bag of purchases onto the passenger seat. "Do you have the time?"

The young man glanced at his watch then up at Rick. "Eight-twenty," he said. His voice was level, but when he saw Rick's face, the expression in his eyes turned from veiled nervousness to surprise, which in turn, was veiled. He stared at Rick for just a moment longer, then he got into his vehicle.

"Wait!" Rick called, stepping between the pumps. "Don't...."

"I gotta go, man," the young man said. "It's not safe here."

"Tell me what's going on," Rick pleaded, but it was too late. The young man slammed the door and roared out onto the road, heading toward the east-bound interstate ramp.

There's no safety in that direction, Rick thought as he finished pumping his gas. He went in to get a cup of coffee for the road, and when the clerk took his money, he gave Rick an appraising look.

"Just passing through?" he asked.

"Going home to Houston," Rick replied, feeling inexplicably guilty.

"You with that young feller was just in here?"

"No," Rick said quickly.

"You was talkin' to him."

"He asked what time it was," Rick said. "That's all."

The clerk gave Rick another calculating expression, with more squint to his eyes. But he didn't say anything else as he handed over the change. Rick hurried out of the store, got in his car, and headed toward the interstate.

Though he'd watched the young man turn east on I-10, Rick didn't see the dark SUV again. Soon, he settled in for the long drive to San Antonio. On the way, he contemplated his options. They seemed even more limited than before. In fact, there was only one, and it was more an inevitable conclusion than an option. He had to go home to Betty and pretend that everything was like it always had been. He had to go to work each morning and home again each night. He had to mow the lawn on Saturday morning and make love to his wife that evening, and maybe they'd go out to eat or to a movie. And somehow, he had to learn to distinguish individuals among all those similar faces.

After spending the night in San Antonio and relaxing in front of the TV, he felt better. He knew he'd made the right decision. It would be all right. He'd learn to fit in. In the morning, he looked at himself in the mirror while he shaved and thought he looked better than he had the day before—like he might fit in. He grabbed a quick breakfast and drove back to Houston.

When he pulled into the driveway of his home, Betty was inside, watching TV. He went in, and after he put his suitcase in the bedroom, he joined her in the den.

"What's on?" he asked.

"*The Punctilios,*" she said. It was her favorite show, all about Myra and Tom Punctilio and their misadventures in married life.

Betty looked different. Better.

"Did you do something to yourself ?" he asked. "Maybe you hair?"

"No," she said, eyes glued to the screen. "I'm just the same old me."

"Yes," he said, sitting down next to her on the sofa. "I think I'll watch, too."

"It's a good one," she said. "Myra thinks Tom will like it if she cooks his steak a different way, but you know that Tom will only eat his steak grilled to perfection with his favorite steak sauce."

"Now, why would she do that?" Rick asked.

"That's what's so silly," Betty said. "Shhh. Look. She's about to serve it to him, and he doesn't know."

Rick had to admit that it was pretty funny, but he didn't laugh aloud. Instead, he only smiled because his face felt a little stiff.

MEETINGS WITH ARTHUR

PLAYING TAG AROUND THE SCHOOL yard was a real obsession for me in third grade. My sister, Amy, was four years older than me and scorned such childish games. Since she went to the big school next door to the one I went to, and I thought she was wise in the ways of the world, I was a bit hurt by her offhand attitude toward my favorite pastime. Though I often tried to get back at her by making fun of her stuffed animal collection or her friends, I never really seemed to get much satisfaction. But despite her disparagement, I couldn't help but talk about the game to her as we rode home on our bicycles each afternoon.

The way home lay over a hill and down a valley, two or so miles. By injunction of our parents, we always rode together. I guess they must have felt we were safer that way. Or at least that I was safer. The arrangement was fine except when one of us had to stay after school. Then the other had to wait, too. As I was primarily the one kept late for minor infractions, Amy was justifiably grumpy on such occasions. On the day the business with the train started, we were running late for just such a reason, though not terribly so. Just the same, Amy was as angry as if I'd had to stay later. The reason was that if we didn't beat the 3:45 freight, we'd have to spend several minutes waiting for the train to pass. Naturally, this would put us home even later than ever, and Amy would miss most of her favorite afternoon TV program.

"Come on, you dodo," she said to me. "Hurry, or we'll get caught by the train."

We were pushing our bikes up the long hill from the school. That was the hardest part of the trip. Once we reached the top, we could coast down the other side, cross the railroad tracks at the bottom, then ride down the road that paralleled the tracks until we reached our home street. The way wasn't difficult, and the only thing that could go wrong would be a train blocking us.

We reached the top of the hill, and as we mounted our bikes, we looked to see if the train was coming. Though the road that led to the bottom was winding for most of its length, and the bottom was hidden from a viewer at the top, there was a portion of track that could be seen through a break in the trees and houses covering the slope of the hill. This section of track was down to the left of where we stood, and about three-quarters of a mile away. The train would pass across this section of track before it reached the crossing at the bottom of the hill, and if we could see it through this perspective window, then we could be certain we'd have to wait for it to pass when we got to the bottom.

No train was visible, and Amy shouted to me to come on. Then she started down the hill, pedaling at first, then braking as her momentum built up. I followed as fast as I could, but I was still a novice bike rider, cautious of the steepness of the hill and the many turns. Amy was soon out of sight, though I tried to keep up with her.

About half way down the hill was another perspective window, showing another section of track, a bit closer to the road crossing. As I looked through this, I saw the train passing by. I slowed down, not so much from a realization that I could never beat the train to the crossing as to avoid Amy's wrath for as long as possible. When I finally did reach the bottom, I found Amy sitting on the curb, waiting for me, watching the train clack by. I sat next to her, ignoring the nasty look she shot in my direction.

"Could you play tag with a train, Amy?" I asked, forgetting her anger after a few moments. She gave me a withering look that only an older sibling can give.

"Don't be silly, you dodo."

I didn't think the question was silly, but prudently decided to keep my mouth shut. Shortly after, the train rumbled by, and the clanging bell and flashing light ceased. We hopped on our bikes and rode for home.

By the time we reached there, I'd forgotten all about the train, and raced in to turn on my favorite cartoon show, which came on after Amy's favorite. Amy usually joined me, though she professed to be too old for such childish fare, but not this time. I didn't miss her until the commercial break started trying to convince me to convince my mother to buy a certain brand of crystallized sugar masquerading as corn flakes. I thought Amy might be in the kitchen getting a snack or something and wandered in to look for her. She wasn't there, but I could see her outside, sitting on the back step. When I pushed open the screen, she didn't even turn around to look at me.

"*Flu Flu and Crazy Dog* is on, Amy."

"So what?"

"Don't you want to watch?"

"Not today, Michael."

"Watcha doin'?"

"Thinking."

"Well, I'm going back in and watch *Flu Flu and Crazy Dog*," I told her, and I let the screen door slam shut in emphasis as I retreated to the TV room. I was puzzled by her behavior, but soon got lost in the cartoons and thought no more on it.

The following day after school, I was running around with some of my classmates, playing tag of course, and waiting for Amy to find me so we could ride home. She was later than usual when she came out the door and waved to me. I ran over, pulling to a panting stop in front of her.

"Where were you?" I asked.

"Inside," she answered enigmatically. "Come on, let's go."

"We're gonna get caught by the train," I said to her, trying to make the statement as caustic as possible. To my surprise, Amy merely shrugged and walked off to the bicycle rack. Despite her nonchalance, I sensed an underlying stiffness, and, on the way out of the school yard, I asked what was wrong. Was she in trouble with her teacher?

No, she told me. There was no trouble. What was it, then? Why had she stayed after school? She was talking to a friend, she told me, then said to shut up and stop asking questions. I did so, pedaling quietly behind her until we had to dismount to walk up to the top of the hill.

As we rounded the top, Amy stopped and mounted her bike. I got a running start on mine and with a few furious pedals was past her, starting down the hill toward the railroad tracks. I reached the first curve before I realized Amy wasn't behind me. Skidding to a halt, I looked back to see her straddling her bike at the top of the hill, her gaze directed down the hill to her left.

"Come on, Amy!" I shouted and waved for her. She ignored me, or maybe she didn't hear me. I yelled again, and this time, whether she heard me or not, she stepped on the pedal, and her bike began to roll down the hill. I watched her descend, but instead of slowing as she reached me, she kept pedaling right on past, down the hill. Yelling for her to wait, I followed as fast as I dared. I passed the second place where the train tracks could be seen, saw the train already moving down them, and called out the fact to Amy. But she was disappearing around the next bend, and I didn't see her again until I got to the bottom. She was straddling her bike, watching the train go past. Her face was flushed, a strange light in her eyes. Ignoring my questions, she watched the last of the train pass, then we remounted and rode home.

Thus began a pattern that took me the better part of the week to figure out. Each day, Amy would hang around after school, doing what, I wasn't sure. Then she'd come to drag me from my tag game, and we'd ride home. At the top of the hill, she'd wait until she could see the train pass through the perspective window, then she'd ride furiously to the bottom where the road crossed the tracks. Being such a tag fanatic, I soon realized she was racing the train, but the reasons were obscure to me.

"Are you playing tag with the train?" I asked her on about the fourth day we waited at the top of the hill for the train to show itself.

"Sort of," she replied distantly, her attention on the perspective window.

"Why don't you just play with the rest of us at school?"

"Because this is different," she said, for once taking her attention off the visible portion of track and looking right at me. I was a bit taken aback by the intensity of her gaze, but I could tell she wasn't angry or anything like that, just excited in a way I'd never seen before.

"How?" I wanted to know, but didn't get an answer.

"Darn!" she exclaimed and began pumping her bike down the hill. I saw that the train was visible below, and I chased behind, realizing I couldn't catch up with her. In moments, she was out of sight around the next bend. I finally pulled up next to her at the bottom, with the train already half past.

"I'm sorry, Amy," I said, feeling guilty for having distracted her. Again she turned that new look on me, and again I saw she wasn't angry.

"It's okay," she said, and we started home.

Mother noticed we weren't coming home as quickly as we used to, and questioned us about it. Amy told her she was staying late to help a friend with a special project, and that I occupied myself playing tag until she was through. She didn't mention the train, so I thought I would.

"That's right," I cut in. "And every day we're just late enough to get caught by the train."

Amy shot me a look that Mom didn't see but that spoke volumes to me. It told me I'd better keep my mouth shut about the train. But Amy needn't have worried, for Mom didn't notice anything unusual. She was aware that the train passed daily through the valley, and if we were a little late we'd have to wait for it. She'd cautioned us enough times to keep back when we did, for the crossing had no barrier, only a warning light and bell.

But if Mom didn't suspect Amy was racing the train, she did begin to suspect something else—something I didn't understand at the time, though I was aware of the basic differences between boys and girls. Amy had been racing the train to the bottom of the hill for about a month when I chanced to overhear Mom asking her some questions one night before bedtime.

She asked about the friend Amy was staying after school to help. I held my breath, for I was fairly sure Amy wasn't actually staying after school to help anyone, though I really didn't know what she did until we left. However, Amy came right out with the name Arthur. She and Arthur, she said, were working together on a science fair project. Mom seemed to think all her questions were answered then and there, and though she did ask what the project was, I could tell she wasn't as curious about it as she was about Arthur.

I was sure Amy had lied about meeting someone named Arthur, so I decided to see for myself what she did after school each day. The next afternoon, I sacrificed my tag time and went in search of her. I wasn't very familiar with the big school where the older kids attended class, and I got lost until a teacher saw me and, perhaps suspicious that a younger kid would be wandering around where he didn't belong, asked me what I was doing. I told her I was looking for my sister, and she showed me how to get to the wing where the seventh-grade classes were. I was soon in the right hall, and presently found Amy. I was surprised when I did. There was a boy with her.

They were at the back of the classroom, where a lot of projects were set up on tables and counters. Several other students were in the room, all engaged in their projects. I sidled into the room and over to Amy. When she saw me, her face turned red. To this day, I'm not sure if it was her boyfriend she was embarrassed by or me. Maybe it was a combination of the two, but whatever it was, she hurried me out of the room and in a sharp but hushed voice told me to go back to my friends until she came and got me. I did, only slightly perturbed at her attitude. I'd gotten a good look at the boy she was with and was more concerned with him than with Amy's scolding. I don't suppose there were any distinguishing features to him, though. He was just an older kid, taller than me, slightly long legged, with a some-what thin face and brown hair.

I did go back to where my friends were playing tag but didn't feel like joining in. I was wondering about Amy, Arthur, and the train. Before I knew about Arthur, I'd thought Amy was just staying after school as an excuse to be late enough to race the train. But if Amy had reasons for staying after school other than the train, why was she racing it? This was an imponderable question for me, and I re-solved to discover the answer. When Amy finally came by to collect me, I almost blurted out an interrogation right then but stopped myself. She wouldn't have answered, or worse, she'd have given misleading answers. I'd have to discover the truth on my own.

That afternoon, however, I didn't have a chance to ask or observe anything. I don't know if Amy was angry with me for seeking her out, or if something else was bothering her, but whatever the reason, instead of waiting for the train at the top of the hill and racing to the bottom, she just rode down the hill, letting me keep up with her. The train had nearly passed, and we waited in silence for it to clear the crossing. When we reached home, she went straight to her room and stayed there until dinner. And after we'd eaten, she returned to her room and occupied herself there until it was time to go to bed.

The next morning, on the way to school, she seemed to be a little melancholy, but that evening she beckoned me from my tag game with her normal spirits. We rode to the hill and pushed our bikes up it. There we paused, both of us looking though the perspective window at the train tracks running through the valley below. While we waited for the appearance of the train, I saw Amy pull a shiny, pendulous object from her pocket.

"What's that?" I asked, leaning forward for a closer look.

"A stopwatch," she replied then told me what it was for.

"Where'd you get it?" I asked in a hushed voice. "Did you steal it?"

"I didn't steal it, you dodo!" she retorted huffily. "I borrowed it from Arthur."

"Yeah," I shot back, not to be undone. "Well, I bet he stole it."

"He did not! He got it from his father, who's the gym coach at the high school."

"What's a gym coach?"

"He teaches recess, sort of," she told me, and I knew then I had her over a barrel.

"Hah! There's no such thing as a recess teacher!" I replied nastily. Amy just looked at me like I was an idiot, though, and I was cowed. I wanted to hold the stopwatch, but Amy refused, saying I'd probably break it or lose it or something.

"Whatcha got it for?" I wanted to know.

"You'll see."

A moment later we heard the distant rumble that heralded the approach of the train. Amy watched the tracks intently, and, as the train approached, her thumb pressed down on the stem of the stopwatch. Then she was off, racing down the hill, with me dropping behind. As I neared the crossing at the bottom of the hill a couple of minutes later, I saw Amy there, examining the stopwatch. I rode over to her and made a rude noise.

"Wassamatter? You break it?

She ignored me and finished her examination.

"What time does it say?" I asked, edging over to her. She held up the watch dramatically for me to see but snatched it back before I could actually do so, stuffing it into her pocket.

"Come on, Amy," I whined.

"It says it's time to go home," she replied, hopping on her bike and pedaling away. Yelling something derogatory after her, I followed at a safe distance.

For the next two weeks, I watched as Amy timed the train's run from the spot on the tracks visible through the perspective window to the crossing at the bottom of the hill. She also calculated her own time from the top to the crossing. The train usually took eighty-three seconds to cover the distance, and Amy's best time was ninety-eight seconds. She consented to let me check my own time down the hill, but I couldn't do it in less than two minutes. Shortly after that, the stopwatch disappeared. I suppose she gave it back to Arthur. Then, for more than three weeks, she left me at the top of the hill to follow at my slower pace while she raced to the bottom in pursuit of her unuttered goal.

During this time, Mom asked me what was going on with Amy. Did I know Arthur? I answered as best as I could without revealing Amy's activities. I knew that racing with the train was dangerous and that Mom wouldn't approve, so I skirted the subject. I told her I'd seen Arthur though I hadn't actually met him. I mentioned he was the son of the recess teacher at the big school, and she gave me a curious look but didn't ask more.

Mom's questions made me a little nervous about Amy's activities. Perhaps they forced me to think more about what she was doing, about the possible dangers involved, or maybe I was just concerned about having to hide the truth from our parents for Amy's sake. Whatever the reasons, I confronted her with my fears one day while we waited at the top of the hill for the train. To my chagrin, she all but ignored me, putting off my objections with either a shrug or glib answers that I couldn't refute. I was getting quite frustrated when the train appeared and Amy took off, racing down the hill and out of sight around the first bend.

Angry and hurt, I resolved to play no further part in Amy's foolishness. She could race the train all day and night if she wanted, but I planned to ignore her. Thereafter, for several weeks, when we got to the top of the hill, Amy would wait for the first view of the train then race to the bottom, but I merely continued to ride on to the crossing, not waiting for Amy to begin. About half the time she sped by me on the slope, and the other half I watched her skid to a stop at the crossing just moments after the train rumbled across the road. And I couldn't help but notice she kept arriving at the crossing a bit sooner each day. By the end of that period, Amy was coming around the last bend in the road just as the train crossed.

Then one day, I watched Amy slide to a stop in front of the crossing only a second after the locomotive roared through. Despite myself, my interest renewed. Excitedly, I ran over to where she sat on her bike, watching the train pass. Her face was impassive as I plucked at her sleeve and went on about how close she'd come that time. She all but ignored me as the train rumbled on. Then she turned her eyes on me but looked right through me, not seeming to hear what I said. I was hurt by her disregard, but as we left the crossing and rode home, I thought of the weeks I'd meanly neglected her efforts. By the time we got home, I apologized to Amy, and though she nodded and smiled, I could tell her attention was elsewhere.

The following day she failed to race the train. We arrived at the top of the hill about the usual time, but instead of waiting there for the train to appear, Amy just leisurely coasted down the hill to the crossing. Puzzled, I followed, calling out questions but getting no replies. When we reached the bottom the train was already well through the crossing. As we braked in front of the tracks, I asked her again why she wasn't racing. This time she looked at me and shrugged, saying she wasn't interested. I wanted to know how that could be after all the time and effort she'd expended, but she merely said she just didn't feel like it.

The next few weeks were bleak ones for me. I'd had my own interest and excitement renewed by Amy's near victory, and the fact that she'd stopped racing was a blow to me, especially since I saw myself responsible. I believed that if I hadn't ignored her efforts for the weeks I had, she'd still be racing the train. At last, after all the self-recriminations, it struck me that maybe Amy was scared.

"Chicken" was a popular epithet around grade school, but it was another thing to apply it to one's older sibling. I shied away from the realization for several days, even though I'd begun to understand there might be something to fear. I remembered the dead dog Amy and I had found in the weed-filled ditch between the road and the train tracks the year before. We'd stopped to stare at the mangled and already bloating body for several minutes, wondering what had happened. It had been hit by a car or a train, but we couldn't decide which. The body remained in the ditch until it completely decomposed—an instructive but fascinatingly unsightly and odorous lesson in biology. Thoughts of the dog preyed on my mind for a week until they burst out one afternoon.

"Amy," I panted, pushing my bike faster to catch up with her as we trudged up the hill. "Amy, are you afraid of the train? The dog...."

She shot a curious look at me that shut me up but said nothing until we reached the top of the hill. There, for the first time in weeks, she stopped and stared toward the perspective window.

"I don't think so, Michael," she said, not looking at me but at the visible lines of the tracks far down the hill. "I don't think I'm afraid. Do you?" She turned and asked the last of me, but I found it difficult to answer. I was confused by my own thoughts, not willing to trust my mouth to say the right thing. Apparently she sensed my confusion, for she turned away and again stared at the tracks.

"Come on," she said, urgency tingeing her voice. "Let's watch the train cross the road." She started down, but not so fast I couldn't keep up.

We got to the bottom in time to watch the train rush through, and as it went by, I couldn't help but feel awed by its size and power. Amy had an incomprehensible look on her face, in her eyes, as the cars thundered down the track.

Two days later, she started racing again. I was elated despite my fears, except for one thing. She wouldn't allow me to be at the bottom when she got there. I had to promise to remain at the top of the hill until the train first appeared and only start down the hill after she did. At first, I believed she was trying to punish me for my inconsideration and indifference the month before. Then it came to me that perhaps she wanted to be alone in her effort, that she didn't consider what she was doing to be a spectator sport. Only later did I realize she was protecting me in case she failed.

I was irked by the restriction, but she was adamant, so there was little I could do but comply. Even so, I knew, despite the fact that I couldn't actually see, that over the next month she gradually came closer to the tracks each time she arrived at the crossing. She took on a single-minded intensity after leaving the school each day that didn't ease until she'd raced to the bottom of the hill.

Then, one night after Mom and Dad had put us to bed, when I'd nearly fallen asleep, I heard someone softly enter my room and come over to my bed. I rolled over to see Amy standing there, silhouetted by the half-light from the door. She was dressed in pajamas, her hair slightly disheveled.

"Michael," she said quietly. "I have something for you."

"What is it?" I was puzzled, for Amy wasn't in the habit of giving me things except for birthday and Christmas presents.

She reached out her hand, and I took the object from her. I instantly knew what it was, and as I held it up to the light, I was even more puzzled and not a little frightened. It was something I'd coveted and had tried to trade for on many occasions. She'd never relented, though, and that made her presentation all the more curious.

"What's it for?" I asked, not daring to say more.

"It's for you," she said with a slight catch in her breath. "You always liked it, and I want you to have it."

"Thanks, Amy," I said lamely, feeling lost.

"I love you, Mikey," she said, bending over to hug me. Then she turned quickly and went out of the room. I lay there for some time, holding the prism up to the light from the half-opened door, watching bands of color sparkle in the glass. Still grasping the prism in my fist, I fell asleep.

The next day, Amy came to get me after school. I wasn't playing tag but was sitting on a bench, waiting for her, fingering the prism and holding it up to the sun. When Amy came up, I stuffed the prism into my pocket and followed her to the bike racks. We left the school yard and rode to the hill. We walked to the top, neither of us speaking. I sensed that today was different from yesterday. The race was going to be for real. The prism was angular in my pocket, reminding me with every step I took of every time I'd hurt my sister. I tried to speak to her, but she wasn't listening. At the top of the hill, I took out the prism, held it up to the sun, and sprayed a rainbow onto Amy's back, showering her with color. Then her back was gone, and she was pedaling furiously down the hill.

"Amy!" I cried out. "Amy!" I stuffed the prism into my pocket and took off after her. She rounded the first bend in the road and was lost to sight.

A great dread rose in me as I gave chase. Visions of the dead dog, torn and smelly in the ditch, rushed past with the scenery as I raced to the bottom of the hill, crying out Amy's name. Tears streaked my cheeks, and I was shaking so hard I could barely steer around the curves. At last, after what seemed like forever, I reached to bottom of the hill and skidded to a halt in front of the tracks.

The train was rumbling through the crossing, but of Amy there was no sign. I looked around frantically, thinking she might be off to the side, but still I couldn't see her. I had two thoughts, then, conflicting but equally terrible. One was of Amy ascending from the Earth, dressed in white wings; the other was of her crouching behind a bush or a tree somewhere on the slope above me, snickering at the stupidity of her little brother. Anger ran through my fear like hot lightning through a dark cloud. Then, as I turned to look at the train, I saw her.

She lay on the ground on the other side of the tracks, unmoving. Her bike was several feet away, one wheel spinning around and around. I moved as close to the train as I dared and peered beneath the rushing, clattering cars, fear wiping away all anger. She was on her back, but twisted slightly to one side. One of her arms was thrown across her face, and I could see blood on one of her knees.

"Amy!" I screamed beneath the train, but the clanging bell and rumbling rattle wiped out my tiny voice.

The train never seemed to take so long to pass, though it must actually have done so in a couple of minutes or less. By the time it had, I was frantic with panic. As the caboose went by, I raced across the rails to her. Yes, there was definitely blood on her. I plunged to the ground beside her, took her arm in my shaking hands, and lifted it from her face. To my intense relief, her eyes were open, and as I sat back on my haunches and began to bawl out in great huffs, she turned them on me and a small smile crossed her lips. Then she sat up and hugged me to her.

"It's all right, Mikey," she said again and again. "It's all right. It's over with. It's over."

At last she pushed me back and examined the scrape on her knee. Seeing it wasn't much, she turned back to me. I'd stopped bawling, though I was still snuffling and leaking from the eyes.

"Get your bike," she said. As I did, she picked up her own and waited for me to come back across the tracks.

EXPIRATION DATE

THE WAITING ROOM WAS WARM and stuffy, and the air, redolent with the odors of dozens of impatient, nervous people, was hard to breathe.

Adam plucked at his collar and shuffled his feet. It was more movement than he'd experienced for ten minutes. What the hell was keeping them? He craned to the left and stared down the line, but it snaked around the corner ahead like a long but multipalegic centipede. Somewhere beyond that was a counter where a bored civil servant processed the cross section of humanity queued up.

Or should be processing.

Adam glanced at his watch. Eleven minutes since the line had moved a single step.

Crap. At this rate, he was going to be here all morning, and all he had to look forward to this afternoon was sitting in the waiting room at the mechanic's. Why the hell had that cop stopped him?

He stared out into the waiting room, where row after row of uncomfortable plastic chairs sat in lines bolted together and bolted to the floor. Most of the chairs were filled, and a lot of the people were filling out forms. He glanced to the right. Signs in English gave the preliminary instructions, followed by the same instructions in Spanish and Vietnamese: "All visitors must check in at the visitors' check-in desk."

He was in the line for the check-in desk, but he was pissed that he had to be here at all. Why had that damn cop noticed that his license plate was expired? That had been what started this waste of time. And to compound matters, when the cop pulled him over and walked up to the driver's door, he'd seen that the car's inspection sticker was out. And when he'd looked over Adam's license, he'd simply commented that the license was expired, too, and had written him up for that, as well. Then he'd asked for proof of insurance.

Adam knew that wasn't up-to-date, either. His old insurance company had dropped him, and he hadn't had the time to search out another. Besides, he always drove carefully, and he'd never been in a wreck. Insurance was just a big protection racket, anyway.

"Get 'em fixed before the court date," the cop said after handing the four tickets to Adam, "and the judge'll probably dismiss the charges."

"Thanks," Adam replied, thinking, you could have just given me a warning, you bastard. After all, the inspection sticker and licenses were just oversights on Adam's part. He'd been so busy lately that he barely had time to eat much less pay attention to bullshit like license plate, inspection sticker, and driver's license expiration dates.

That had been yesterday, so today, Adam was going to take care of everything before he got stopped again and the tickets piled up. At least, he hoped it would all be done today. He couldn't afford to miss another day at work. The boss was already on his case to finish the paperwork for the Joiner account. But if this damn line didn't start moving, he'd never make it to the mechanic's in time to get the inspection.

At last, the line moved. Slowly. Creepingly slowly. But it did move. Eventually, he crept around the corner and up to the check-in desk.

"New or renewal?" asked the bored-looking woman behind the counter. She was wearing a Department of Public Safety uniform, but it didn't look like she'd ever been on patrol. She was slender and tiny—under five feet, Adam judged, though she was perched on a stool.

"Renewal, I guess," Adam said. "My license expired."

"Do you have your old license with you?"

"Right here." Adam dug it from his wallet and passed it over.

She looked at it a moment, then her fingers clicked on her computer keyboard. She stared at the screen the shook her head and handed the license back.

"Birth certificate."

"What?"

"I'll need to see your birth certificate, Mr. Zachary."

"Why?" Adam was dumbfounded. "Can't I just renew my license?"

"Not this time. It's been more than six months. You need to bring in a birth certificate or passport."

"But…," Adam began helplessly, but the look in the DPS officer's eyes told him there were no buts.

He stuck his wallet back into his pocket and headed for the door. Well, there went tomorrow morning, at least. He'd find his birth certificate tonight and come back tomorrow first thing. But right now, he was going to get the inspection sticker taken care of.

"Proof of insurance," the mechanic told him.

"Proof of insurance?" Adam was puzzled until he remembered that you had to have proof of insurance before you could get your car inspected.

"I forgot it," he said. "I'll come back tomorrow."

There was a quickie insurance company on the main drag near his apartment, and he drove over there.

"Driver's license," the woman at the desk said.

He handed it over, feeling self-conscious, and she handed it right back.

"This is expired, Mr. Stuart," she said. "I can't issue a policy without a valid driver's license."

"I'll come back tomorrow," he told her.

It was only early afternoon, but Adam felt like he'd been busting his ass all day, and he'd gotten absolutely nothing done. I'll just go home, he thought. Get there before rush hour starts. Find that damn birth certificate, eat, watch the tube, try to relax a little.

He made it home without picking up another ticket.

The apartments he lived in were pretty run down, and there wasn't any covered parking, so he just found a spot as close as he could get to his building, which was pretty far away since the lot was full of the junkers owned by his ne'er-do-well neighbors. He slalomed his way down a sidewalk littered with faded, broken toys, up the rusting iron stairs to his landing, and into the hot humidity of his apartment.

He hated not keeping his AC on when he wasn't in the apartment, but he just couldn't afford it these days. It was pretty frustrating.

And his frustrations for the day weren't over. He couldn't find his birth certificate. He knew it should be in his files, but it just wasn't there.

"God damn her!" he spat.

It had to have been Gloria. Where the hell was it if she hadn't taken it when she left? Oh, not on purpose. She didn't like him anymore, but she wasn't the vindictive sort. She probably just grabbed a bunch of papers she thought were hers and hadn't bothered to go through them to see that some of his stuff was mixed in.

He picked up the phone and dialed her number. He had to look it up in his Rolodex because it had been so long since they'd spoken.

"You've reached the number of Gloria Speranza," her voice mail voice said brightly. "Please leave a message."

She hadn't sounded that good when he'd been married to her, Adam thought. And he couldn't help but feel a twinge of pain at the fact that she'd reverted to her maiden name.

"Gloria. This is Adam. I think you accidentally took some of my stuff out of the file drawer when you left. My birth certificate, at least. I need it pretty badly. See if you've got it, and give me a call. Thanks."

He hung up and stared at the phone, then into space. Then he shrugged.

Might as well eat, he thought. Nothing else I can do right now, anyway. He went into the kitchen, but there really wasn't much in there he could scrounge into anything resembling a meal. He'd been too busy to go shopping, and he'd been eating out a lot lately.

He thought about going out to get something, but the idea of driving around with an expired license, inspection sticker, and license plate and no insurance gave him pause. The pause didn't outlast the grumbling of his stomach. What the hell choice did he have?

He locked his apartment and went down to the parking lot. But when he started his car, he noticed that he was nearly out of gas. No matter. He could stop at the gas station on his way to eat.

A few minutes later, he pulled up next to the pumps at a convenience store, got out of his car, and slipped his debit card into the slot in the pump. The LCD screen asked for his code, and he typed it in. The pump's internal computer chewed on his number for a while, then suddenly informed him that the card was expired.

He pulled it out, held it up, and peered at it. Sure enough, it had expired the last day of last month, which was yesterday.

"What the…?"

He didn't finish the expletive because he was too dumbfounded. Why hadn't the bank sent him a new card like they usually did? That was part of their job, wasn't it? How did they expect their customers to keep up with every little date? They were the ones with the supercomputers that knew everything. All he had was his human memory.

He stuck the debit card back into his wallet and pulled out his sole credit card. All the others had been cancelled by the various banks since Gloria had charged them to the max before she'd left him, and he hadn't been able to keep up with the payments. In fact, he'd been dodging phone calls from creditors for months now. It had gotten so bad, he was afraid to answer the phone, and all he ever did any more was automatically erase all the messages on his voice mail without listening to any of them. It didn't really matter since no one ever called him for personal reasons. It seemed that all the friends he and Gloria once had were really Gloria's friends.

He looked suspiciously at the card. He couldn't remember if it was maxed out, too, or if he had a little cushion before he reached his credit limit. Well, there was only one way to find out.

He stuck the card into the slot.

Moments later, the LCD read that he was over his limit.

Feeling suddenly tired, he pulled out the card, put it back into his wallet, and checked his cash. A single $20 bill was there —enough for tonight if he only spent $10 on gas and ate at a fast food joint. He went inside the station, gave the attendant the $20, got his change, and went back outside to pump his gas. The $10 didn't buy much, and when he started the engine, the gas gauge barely seemed to move. He ate at a burger joint, then went home, suppressing his growing indigestion.

At home, he discovered that he was out of antacids. He had enough cash to buy some, but rather than drive to the corner convenience store, he walked. The purchase left him with exactly one dollar.

When he got home, he was bushed. He plumped down in front of the TV, but in the end, he couldn't concentrate worth a damn because his mind kept churning over how he'd let so much of his life slide. What else had gone by the wayside? He turned off the TV and went into the bedroom, where his wallet lay on the dresser. He picked it up, went to the bed, sat down, and began emptying everything onto the rumpled blanket.

The expired driver's license and insurance card and the useless debit and credit cards started one pile—things he might need the numbers for. He began another pile with his old voter's registration card. It was linked to the precinct where his house had been. The house he'd shared with Gloria. But he hadn't bothered to reregister since he'd moved, so the card was so much trash now. So was his health insurance card, since the insurance plan had been Gloria's and he'd been riding along as spouse. The second pile started to build up as he added cards that had been pretty much meaningless the moment he'd acquired them. There were two restaurant loyalty cards that promised a free meal after the purchase of ten meals, both with only two or three boxes stamped; a bookstore discount card he'd bought at the mall just before the bookstore there closed; and a library card that he'd used once about ten years ago.

Hell, he thought. Maybe it's still valid. He picked it up and used it to start a third pile to which he could only add a grocery store rewards card. Now that was still good, he thought. Those things didn't expire.

He threw away everything that had expired except the driver's license, insurance card, and debit and credit cards.

129

These he stuffed back into his wallet with the library card, the grocery store card, and the single dollar bill that was left from the $20 he'd spent earlier in the evening. The wallet felt frighteningly slim, and it nearly slipped through his fingers when he carried it back to the dresser.

He was exhausted. More exhausted than he'd ever felt in his life. It had been a trying day. Maybe he should go to bed early. He had another long day ahead of him, and it would start out poorly with a call to his boss to say he was going to miss another day of work.

In the morning, the call went as badly as he'd anticipated. The tone in his boss's voice indicated that he'd better not be trying to pull a fast one or Adam might as well not come in tomorrow. Or ever again.

Adam fixed himself a cup of coffee, using the last grounds in the can. He had to settle with that for breakfast since there wasn't anything to eat. While he was drinking his coffee, he tried calling Gloria again, but all he got was her voice mail.

After he hung up, he was at a loss what to do. Everything hinged on getting hold of his birth certificate. Without that, he couldn't get a new driver's license, and without that, he couldn't do anything else. He couldn't even go to the bank to arrange for a new debit card because they'd only ask for valid identification, which he didn't have.

Wait a minute! What about his Social Security card? It wouldn't do for ID, but no telling whether or not he might need it. He carried his coffee to his desk and ransacked the drawers, looking for the Social Security card, but it was nowhere to be found. Gloria must have take it, too.

What the hell else did she have that was his? Wasn't it enough she'd left him flat and taken the house and furniture and car and bank account and any credit card that might not be maxed out?

He had to get hold of that birth certificate, and the only way to do that was to get hold of Gloria. He punched in her office number and got her voice mail.

Crap! It looked like he was going to have to go to her office. He hated to do it, but what choice was there? Adam finished his coffee and went down to his car.

One of his taillights was broken. He didn't think it had been broken yesterday. Maybe someone had bumped into him in the parking lot. Or maybe it was that vandalous gang of kids who lived in the complex with their various careless or uncaring parents. Did it matter, really? It was just one more costly headache he'd have to fix before the day was out. Oh, that's right, he thought. He couldn't get it fixed because he couldn't pay for the repair without a debit card.

It was while he was starting the car that he realized the broken light was cause for another sort of concern. It might attract the attention of a cop, who would pull him over and notice his out-of-date license plate and inspection sticker and ask for his expired driver's license and now-trashed insurance card. Adam would have to stay off the main streets, even if it would take him longer to get around. He couldn't afford another traffic stop.

It took him more than an hour to reach Gloria's office building, and then he had to circle the area like a vulture, seeking a free place to park. At last, he did, and he hurried up to her office.

"I'm sorry, sir," the receptionist said, looking at him skeptically. She was new and didn't know who Adam was. "Miss Speranza isn't in. She's out of town and won't be back for two weeks."

Two weeks, Adam thought. Crap.

"It's very urgent that I get in touch with her," he said to the receptionist. "Can you tell me how to reach her?"

"I'm sorry, sir," the receptionist said. "We can't give out personal information."

"Look, I'm her ex-husband. She mistakenly took something of mine during the divorce, and I really need to get it back as soon as possible."

"I'm sorry, sir," the receptionist said. The repetition of those words was beginning to get on Adam's nerves. "There's nothing I can do."

You can give me her goddamn contact information, Adam thought loudly, but he forced himself to calm down. It wouldn't do to get thrown out of here. They might even call the police, who, of course, would ask for his driver's license.

"Can I leave a message?"

"Yes, sir." The receptionist handed him a note pad and a pen.

Adam hastily scribbled a request for Gloria to call him as soon as she got the message, then he returned the pad to the receptionist and left the building.

Back in his car, he made the disconcerting discovery that all the extra driving he'd done this morning had used half of what little gas he'd put in last night. He wondered if he had enough to get home. Maybe he should take the freeway. It would be more direct, even if it was chancier. What the hell if he got a ticket? The alternative was running out of gas before he got home. That would be a real killer.

Keeping enough below the speed limit that he irritated every driver around him, Adam got onto the freeway and headed for home. But he hadn't gone far before he saw a cop car coming up the lane to his left. Before the cop was close enough to see the broken taillight or expired license plate, Adam exited, his heart pounding in his chest and his tongue and mouth dry as a desert.

That was close, he thought, then he realized that he'd never taken this particular exit before. He drove up the feeder road, thinking he'd get back on the freeway at the next entrance ramp. Surely the cop had passed by now. But there was no entrance ramp, and the feeder ended at a one-way road going to the right that ran parallel to some railroad tracks. Another one-way road ran down the opposite side of the tracks, going the other way. Tantalizingly, the feeder continued onward on the other side of the tracks, but there was no crossing. He'd have to go down the one-way road to find a crossing to get over to the other side. He could turn only right, so sighing, he went that way, following the tracks for more than a mile before he found a crossing.

Unfortunately, a train locomotive trailing a long line of cars blocked the crossing. Adam stopped and waited for the train to move so he could get across, but the train just sat there. Adam couldn't see any engineer. In fact, there were no train people at all. He wondered how long he'd have to sit here. The crossing wasn't deep enough to pull his car into, so he just sat on the one-way road, nervously watching his rearview mirror for any approaching vehicles. But the road was strangely empty, and his car was the only one in sight.

Adam peered down the track. The train was very long. So long, he couldn't see any end to it. But he couldn't just sit here idling and burning precious gas. Besides, he was exhausted. All the tensions and frustrations and activity of the past couple of days had worn him down, not to mention the lack of food. He could barely keep his eyes open and his grip on the wheel. All he felt like doing was lying down and going to sleep.

I'll just have to drive until I get to the end of the train, he thought.

He accelerated slowly, following the tracks and looking for the end of the train. The damn thing must be five miles long, he thought. He kept passing crossing after crossing, but all were blocked by boxcars, tankers, or cattle cars.

At last, the caboose came into sight, and Adam breathed a sigh of relief that suddenly caught in his chest. He coughed.

He hadn't had anything to drink for hours, and his throat was as dry as he'd ever felt it. He coughed and coughed, each reflex tearing further at his dehydrated air passages. He couldn't even seem to work up any saliva.

The coughing fit subsided, leaving him even more drained than before, about the time he saw the first crossing that wasn't blocked by the train. It was in terrible condition, and he had to ease his car over to keep from bottoming out or jolting himself senseless. When he got across, he saw that the one-way street that had been on the other side of the tracks before the train blocked his view had vanished, and the street he was on led him into a neighborhood he'd never been in. Before long, he was lost.

It wasn't a neighborhood he wanted to be lost in. It was filled with ramshackle houses with junk cars, decrepit boats, and old, rotting furniture sitting in front yards that were either barren dirt or choked with weeds. The few people he saw were rough looking and obviously destitute. That made him feel panicky, especially since he was nearly destitute himself and the gas gauge in the dashboard was beginning to touch the empty mark. He had to find his way back to the freeway. There'd be a gas station there or something. Or someone. Someone who might help him.

He headed in the direction where he thought the freeway lay, but in a few minutes, he was back at the railroad tracks. At least he'd found the other one-way street that led to the freeway. He turned right, and drove down it, the train now to his left, but he hadn't gone a mile before his car began jolting. A hundred yards later, it gave a sputter and died. He let it roll as far as he could, pulling onto the right shoulder, hoping not to edge into the deep, litter-filled ditch that ran along the road opposite the tracks.

He took stock of himself. He needed gas, but he had no money or credit card to pay for it. All he had was the one lone dollar in his wallet. Maybe there was some change in the glove compartment. He checked, but all he found were several old dried-up ballpoint pens, a ten-year-old city map, and an adhesive bandage that had come loose from its brittle wrapper.

He looked at his watch. It read 11:59.

Man, he thought. It sure seems later than that.

Then he had another thought. His watch!

It was nothing fancy, but maybe he could barter it for some gas. All he needed was a gallon. That would get him home, and then he'd be able to figure out something.

He got out, locked the car, and began trudging down the road toward the freeway. At last, just after he passed the locomotive that blocked the first crossing, he could see the freeway arcing over the railroad tracks dimly in the distance, maybe three miles away. He was about a third of the way there and sweating profusely from the hot sun overhead when he looked at his watch again.

It read 11:59. And the second hand wasn't moving.

Adam tapped the watch sharply with his forefinger, but the second hand remained static. Squinting at the watch, he saw that the date had stopped in mid flip. The watch must have failed last night right at midnight. Funny he hadn't noticed, but then he'd been pretty preoccupied all day.

He looked ahead, toward the freeway overpass, which was still a long way off. Then he looked up at the sun. It was very hot.

Adam felt light headed. He should have eaten something for breakfast. He should have had more to drink than just that coffee. He felt weak and trembly.

He stumbled over to the tracks and sat down on the end of a tie, the train tracks at his back. Another wave of vertigo washed over him, and his chest felt heavy. He slowly slumped onto the rough pebbles beside the tracks and looked at the sky again.

135

I'll just lie here for a while, the thought. Rest.

He tried to swallow, but there was no moisture in his throat. The sun blasted down. He knew he should get up and walk toward the distant feeder, but it didn't seem worth the effort. He had no money or identity card and everything had broken down and it was all too complicated to fix. There was no place to go, nothing to do once he got there, and no one to do it with. It was much easier just to lie here in the sun, even if the sun was so hot it made him feel as if he was melting like ice right into the spaces between the hot pebbles....

Before long, two boys about twelve years old wandered slowly down the tracks. One of them carried a stick that he used to poke at this and that odd thing. He used it to poke at a wallet. Picking up the wallet, he looked inside. There was nothing there but a dollar bill and a couple of old cards.

"Expired," he told his friend, and he dropped the cards. As they fell to the gravel, he took out the dollar and tossed the wallet beside the tracks. "It's hot. Let's go get a Popsicle or something."

He and his companion hurried off down the tracks. A little while later, they passed a broken-down car parked at the side of the road. Nobody was around, so they picked up some rocks from the railroad bed and used them to smash the car windows and headlights before running off, laughing and shouting.

Behind them, with a clatter and banging, the train began to move. When it was gone, nothing moved except a little dust devil swirling in the heat.

THE POOL

"Breit," his mother called. "Fetch a bucket of water from the pool."

Sighing, Breit put down the snare he was working on and grudgingly went into the kitchen to get the bucket. After all, he was nearly a man and soon would join the other men in the fields and woods surrounding the village. It was time for him to stop performing childish chores.

But his heart held no real rancor as his feet found their familiar way through the cluster of houses and across the open ground surrounding the pool. Several of the village women were there with their children, but none of the young ones were of Breit's age group or old enough to do any fetching.

He found a place on the bank, dropped the bucket into the water, and watched the ripples spread out to meet and merge with other ripples from the buckets dipped by the women. The water beneath was crystal clear, and Breit stared into it as the bucket filled, feeling his focus shift from its crystal clarity to his inner, murkier depths.

Breit knew the world. He and his friends had explored enough of it to have seen that it was a very large bowl, like those thrown by the potter Nelek. Even Grandfather had affirmed that was true. But the pool puzzled him. Not the fact that it lay there in the bottom of the bowl that was the world, just as the last of his soup puddled the bottom of his eating bowl. That was natural. Water, it seemed, sought the lowest levels of a thing. What didn't seem natural was the stream that fed the pool. He looked up it until it wrapped out of sight around a rocky bend.

It wasn't that the stream moved. Water seeking the lowest level always moved. It was that the stream existed at all. Where did it move *from*?

"No one knows," Grandfather had said when Breit asked about it. "It is enough that it blesses us and keeps the pool filled so that we and the animals of the world might have water to drink."

In their explorations, Breit and his friends had followed the stream as far as they dared as it wound its way down from the highlands beyond the village. The land grew steeper and rockier and, finally, too far from home to venture further. But still the stream flowed from beyond the next bend.

Was there always a next bend? Breit wondered, but it seemed he would never know, though he often walked miles along the stream's length when he was out setting snares or when he had a day free from chores. The stream went on for far too great a distance to find out where it came from. And soon he would be a man and wouldn't have time for childish adventures. That brought a thought of Nesta, with her flashing dark eyes and developing figure.

Smiling, he hefted the bucket and carried it back to his family's home.

His grandfather had returned from the fields and was putting his tools in the shed beside the house as Breit walked up. Calling a welcome, Breit poured some water into the bowl on the stand beside the front door so his grandfather could wash, then he carried the bucket into the house. A few minutes later, his grandfather came in and went to his room to change from his work clothes.

Feeling restless, Breit told his mother he was going out for a walk.

"Dinner will be ready soon," she warned.

"I'll be back," Breit promised as he went out the door.

He didn't walk far—only to the pool. By now, with the dinner hour approaching and the sun already behind the rim of mountains that surrounded the world, nobody was there. Breit liked this time, its quiet suspension between the activity of day and the sleep of night, when the world was filled with a gray dusk that matched the color of the pool.

Breit sat down and stared into the clear water, his vision tracing the contours of the stones on the bottom even where the water was as deep as he was tall. He knew it was at least that deep because he and some of his friends had sneaked into the water one night, though it was forbidden to do so. One of them—scrawny Earh—had nearly died when he found himself so deep that the water went over his head. But Slean, who was strong and quick, had taken off his trousers and, holding onto one leg, had thrown the other towards Earh's flailing hands. Luckily, Earh caught it, and with Slean and Breit both hauling, they pulled him to shore.

The commotion had drawn people from the houses nearest the pool, and soon after, Slean and Earh's parents and Breit's mother and grandfather showed up. None of the parents said much, though there was some muttering in the small crowd as the boys were taken home.

The next day, the three were called to the Council Room, where the Council of Elders already was gathered. Breit's grandfather was among them, his face severe.

"You know that immersing your body in the pool is forbidden," said Brecc, the leader of the council.

"Yes, sir," the boys answered.

"What have you to say for yourselves?"

None of the boys was anxious to speak, but someone had to say something.

"We just wondered what it would be like, Elder," Breit said. "We didn't mean any harm."

"The pool is the source of life for the world," Noak, another elder, reminded them gruffly. "Nothing can be allowed to sully it."

"I'm sorry," Earh said, hanging his head. "It's all my fault. I was the one who went too deep."

"If Slean and Breit hadn't pulled you out, you would have died," Noak said. "Then what would have happened to the pool? I'll tell you: It would have been rendered impure. Then where would we be? Where would your families be?"

Breit had never thought of the pool quite like that, but with Noak's words came a glimmer of understanding of just how important the pool was to the welfare of the village and the world. Before, it had been a fact of life; now, it was *the* fact of life.

"The pool *has* been sullied," said Arundel, another elder. "Precautions must be taken. The pool will be interdicted for one week to allow the disturbed sediments settle."

Breit was shocked. One week. That was a long time for the village to go without water.

"And atonements must be made," Breit's grandfather said. "You three will stand beside the pool every day and tell anyone who approaches to fill their bucket that they must get their water from the stream instead."

That would be a hardship on many of the villagers. The stream, never very large, slipped down a rocky sluice before it entered the pool, and the nearest place that a bucket could be filled was a tiny basin nearly half a mile from the nearest house. But Breit sighed in relief. At least there would be water.

As the boys were dismissed and filed out of the Council Room, Breit heard Noak say to his grandfather, "You need to watch that boy. He has Arpad's blood."

The next week passed as slowly as any in Breit's life. Their guard duty was not really necessary as everyone in the village already knew of the council's decision, but many people passed, carrying their buckets to the way to the distant basin. Some glared, some stared stoically, and some even smiled, but no one laughed. Carrying a bucket of water half a mile or more was no fun. Breit had to do it himself several times each evening after his guard duty was finished for the day.

But what he really thought on as he stared over the pool for those many long days was the comment that Noak had made to his grandfather—that Breit had Arpad's blood. Of course he had Arpad's blood. Arpad had been his father. *Was* his father, though Arpad no longer was in the world.

And that was the puzzle, too, for Arpad had not died. He'd simply disappeared soon after Breit was born. Vanished as thoroughly and mysteriously as a drop of the pool placed on a stone vanished in the sunlight.

But Noak had meant something different about the blood. Something that went beyond kinship.

The week of punishment passed, and two more, but the question about the blood—and the resurrection of the ones about his father's disappearance—did not go away as easily as the frowns of his neighbors. Then one night after dinner, as he sat beside the pool, thinking about the questions, his grandfather came and sat next to him.

"I thought you'd be sick of looking at this thing by now," Grandfather said with a chuckle.

"Never," Breit said. "I could stare into it forever."

"Yes," Grandfather nodded. "I was that way when I was young, too."

"But not now?"

Breit wondered how his grandfather could forget the beauty of the pool. Would he get that way, too, as he grew older?

"I became interested in a deeper pool." The old man pointed up at the stars winking into wakefulness in the early night.

"I never thought of the sky as a pool," Breit said.

"It's too dark to see the pool clearly right now," Grandfather said, "but you know how you can see little specks and motes suspended in the water?" Breit nodded. "I think the stars are like those little specks floating around out there, but all alight for some reason. And what happens if you put a leaf into the pool?"

Breit well knew. The water flowing into the pool from the stream caused a steady current to circulate, and the current would carry the leaf around the edge of the pool until the leaf sank or somebody plucked it out.

"It goes around and around."

"It is the same up there," Grandfather said. "The stars follow a steady movement that goes a certain way, and the pattern lasts a full year. That is how we elders know when to plant and when to harvest. When the winter winds will blow and when the summers bring warm joy."

"How do you know these things?"

"They are part of being a man of the world. You will learn as you grow older. Some men learn more, and some less, but they all learn."

"I want to learn more."

"Of course," the old man said, and Breit thought he heard a note of sadness in his voice. "It's in your blood."

There was a long silence between them, filled only with the hum of night insects.

"What does it mean, Grandfather?" Breit asked. "That I have the blood? I heard Elder Noak say I have Arpad's blood."

"Of course you have Arpad's blood," the old man said. "He was your father."

"But that's not what Elder Noak meant."

"No," the old man said after a moment. "It's not."

"Elder Noak said it like it's something bad. What happened to my father? Was it something bad?"

"I don't know if it was bad," his grandfather said sadly. "I don't know what happened to him. I don't even know if he's alive or dead."

That gave Breit pause. Not to know if Arpad was alive or dead simply did not seem possible. If he was alive, he would be in the world, and if he was dead, his ashes would be in a nook in the Cave of the Dead. How could there be a state where he was not alive or dead?

"I don't understand, Grandfather."

"Perhaps you will, one day," the old man said, putting an arm around Breit's shoulders and hugging him. "You did say you wanted to learn more."

As the weeks passed and summer moved toward fall, Breit found himself more and more troubled by the uncertainty of Arpad's existence. His own father, suspended in some shadowy realm between the world and death. He tried to visualize what such a state might be, but he couldn't.

But he had to. If he had Arpad's blood and didn't find out, who was to say that the same thing might not happen to him?

The thought filled him with dread, and he began to think of himself as somehow tainted. Like Riska, who had gotten so sick, and then everyone around her got sick until everyone in the world was sick. And it was a bad sickness— much worse than the chills and fever that often came in the winter. By then, Riska was well again, and eventually, so was almost everyone else, though several older people had died. Riska's own mother was one of them. Riska didn't have Arpad's blood, but some people said there was something wrong with her blood.

If there was something wrong with Breit's blood, was he going to make everyone sick?

Just the thought made him feel ill. He'd been younger then, but he remembered how the sickness, coming at the time of the harvest, had imposed great hardship on the village, and he didn't want to be responsible for hurting his people. So he began to spend more and more time out of the village, walking the world for hours, keeping to the uplands and forests, away from the village and the fields.

But always he came back to the stream. Every free day he had, he followed it, each day learning more about its quirks and meanders and each day traveling a little farther. Eventually, however, he came to a steep slope that was blocked at the top by a wall of rock that was very tall. The stream fell straight down it into a pool at the bottom before bubbling into the stream bed and running off toward the village. Going farther would require great effort and special equipment.

He stared up to where the cliff stopped, where it was shadowed by overhanging trees. In the far upper reaches beyond that, rose the rim of the world, dim from distance but looking rocky and foreboding. Somewhere up there the stream was born. Breit swore to himself that one day he would find its source.

But doing so would require him to overcome his growing fears. The first fear was easy enough to wave off. It was the fear of death or injury. Breit was not arrogant, and he knew that death or injury might await him on the way to the top of the cliffs, but like many youth, he also had a great faith in his own ability to overcome obstacles. He might stumble, but certainly, he thought, he would rise again.

The second fear was harder to deal with. It was the fear that the elders of the village would do something to him, something to stop him from going or something to punish him if he did go. Many of the people of the village had been looking at him strangely lately, as if they were warily watching one of the black bears that sometimes came down out of the woods covering the highlands that surrounded the village and formed the lower walls of the world.

The third fear was his greatest—more frightening, even, than broken bones or the censure of people with whom he'd always felt safe and secure. Suppose he found himself climbing higher and higher after an ever-elusive source that always promised to be around the next rock, the next bend, but that, instead, went on and on forever?

"Where have you been?" Slean asked him one day as he returned to the village.

"Exploring," Breit said.

"Exploring what?" Earh asked.

"Oh, nothing, really. Just looking in all the nooks and crannies to see what's there."

"Well, I'm done with exploring," Slean said. "That's for children. Let's go to the dance." He meant the evening dance that followed the village's day-long harvest festival that would take place next week. "Nesta will be there." His eyes glittered slyly at Breit.

"I think she likes you, Breit," Earh said.

"Of course she likes him," Slean said, jabbing Earh in the ribs. "You'd better concentrate on finding a girl to like *you*." He turned to Breit. "You're coming, right?"

"Sure," Breit said, though inside he was reluctant to go. Nesta was beautiful and so full of life that Breit didn't want to taint her with Arpad's blood. His blood.

The day of the festival came. Cooking pits and long trestle tables piled with food were set along two sides of the village square, and games of skill and chance were around the other two. The villagers stood or sat everywhere, and all wore their best clothes and happy faces. The harvest was done, and it had been a good one. They had earned a celebration together before the winter cold kept them indoors.

Breit felt awkward as he entered the square with his friends. He wasn't sure why. Growing up, he'd always loved the harvest festival with the bright music and games and plentiful food. But for some reason, this year he felt pensive, as if all the gaiety around him was little more than a dream from which waking would bring him back to something—a world, a life—that was more real.

He followed Slean and Earh around for most of the afternoon, playing games and watching the younger kids get into the same sorts of trouble he and his friends had gotten in just a few years earlier. As the day wore on, he found himself enjoying things more, especially after Slean managed to purloin a partially empty jar of wine, which the three of them sipped on behind the Zivon's barn. It didn't take much to make them tipsy, so they hid the jar in the woodpile and went back to the celebration.

By now night had fallen. The cooking pits were dying out and lanterns lit the square. Some of the games had been cleared away, and in their place, musicians were setting up and tuning their instruments. Soon, they were playing a light air, and out in the area in front of them, a dozen or so couples danced to the happy music. More would join them before long.

"There's Nesta," Slean said, nudging Breit's arm and pointing with his chin at the group of girls across the square.

"Yes," Breit said. He'd already seen her.

"Are you going to ask her to dance?" Slean asked.

"Maybe," Breit said. "Later."

"Well, maybe later I'll be dancing with her if you aren't careful," Slean warned.

Breit knew the subtle challenge should have stirred his blood, but it didn't. His blood....

"It's okay if you do," he said. "I won't mind."

"Well, I won't mind, either," Slean said. His voice was bantering, but his eyes held a mixture of puzzlement and calculation.

"Go ask her now," Breit said, giving Slean a little push.

"I don't know," Slean said.

"Go on. She'll dance with you. You know she loves to dance."

"You won't be mad?"

"No. Go on."

So Slean went, and Earth said in a troubled voice, "But I thought she likes you, Breit."

"She just thinks she likes me. We're too young to know what we really want."

"Well, I know what I want," Earth said, and he disappeared through the crowd, heading toward the food table on the end, where pies were disappearing as fast as the fading sunlight.

Breit watched Slean angle around the edge of the dancers and walk up to Nesta with a smooth swagger. Breit smiled. He knew his friend well enough to know that beneath the surface, Slean probably was trembling. Then the smile faded as he wondered what lay beneath his own trepidation.

Edging out of the crowd, he made his way back to the Zivon's barn and pulled the jar of wine from the woodpile. Sitting with his back to the barn, he took a few sips, but the wine tasted sour on his tongue. He put the stopper back into the jar's mouth and hid the jar in the woodpile so Slean or Earth could find it if they wanted more. Then he slipped between the houses, heading toward the only place he really wanted to be right now.

He sat in his favorite spot by the pool and stared across the surface, where ripples brought by a slight cool breeze were highlighted by the full moon. He watched the water for a long time. Soon it would be winter, and in the winter, the flow of the stream diminished greatly. Breit wondered why that was so. He knew that the melting snow made the stream greater in early spring, but why should the flow be less just because the weather was cold? It made him want to find the stream's source all the more.

Then he stared up, into the void above, where the lights of the fainter stars were washed out or hidden entirely by the brightness of the moon. The harvest moon.

Was that part of the wisdom of the elders—knowing that this moon was the one for the harvest, just as they knew by the stars when to plant seeds in the spring? It made Breit want to know more, and he wondered if knowing more about the void above would fill the emptiness in his own heart. The heart that pumped his blood. Arpad's blood.

A sound came from behind him. It could have been the rustle of drying leaves shaken by the breeze or the scuttle of a night creature hurrying from brush to rock, but he knew it wasn't. He turned and watched a shadowed figure approaching his spot. As the figure neared and passed through a patch of clear moonlight, he saw it was Riska.

"Oh!" she said, as she came up to the water's edge and finally saw him. "Breit?" She seemed surprised. "I'm sorry. I didn't know anyone was here."

She turned to leave, but Breit said, "I don't mind if you stay. I was just sitting here."

"Are you sure? I don't want to make you sick."

She sounded pensive, maybe because many of the villagers felt uncomfortable in her presence after the illness that she'd started.

"I don't mind. Grandfather says that was just a passing thing, anyway. People get sick all the time, and it doesn't have anything to do with them, just with the sickness."

She sat on a nearby rock, and they were silent for a long time. At last she broke the silence, her voice cautious, as if she didn't want to offend.

"You're not thinking of going into the pool, are you?"

The question surprised him, and at first, he didn't know what to say. Then, all he could do was laugh.

"No," he said. "I don't think I'll try that again."

"I'm glad. That whole week the people collected water from the basin, I had to wait until it was nearly dark to get water for my father and me."

"But why?"

"Unless you hadn't noticed, ever since I got sick and Mother died, Father and I have been banished to the cottage near the stream."

Breit knew that. The cottage was the outermost house of the village and one of the poorest.

"What has that to do with when you get your water?"

"Tell me, Breit. Do you spend a lot of time beside the pool?"

"Yes. I like it here."

"When was the last time you saw me here?"

"Why...." He was about to say, unthinkingly, as often as I see anybody, but then he thought about it.

"Not in a long time," he conceded. "Don't they let you come to the pool?"

"They would, I suppose, though many wouldn't like it. But the cottage is closer to the basin, so I draw all our water from there. It's easier to get it directly from the stream than walk all the way down here and back every day."

"I see now," Breit said. "With everybody going to the basin, you were crowded out."

"There you have it," she said, leaning against the rock at her back. As she did, her upper body came into a patch of moonlight, and Breit saw her more clearly.

She was his own age, but the fact hadn't really struck him until this moment. Maybe because he so rarely saw her, he tended to think of her as much younger. But her breasts didn't fit with that image, nor did her features, which were, if not as pointedly beautiful as Nesta's, smooth and lovely.

"Why aren't you at the festival?" she asked.

He didn't want to tell her that he felt more lonely there than he did here alone by the pool.

"I think I drank too much wine," he said.

"You don't seem drunk."

"And you've seen a lot of drunks, have you?"

"One's enough. My father drinks himself to sleep every night. He hates me and blames me for Mother's death and his isolation from the rest of the people. If he drinks, he doesn't have to think about it or me."

"Oh." Breit hadn't known that anyone could be like that. "I'm sorry."

"Don't be. I used to blame myself, but when you live apart from the rest of the people, you get to watch them in ways you couldn't if you lived in their midst. I've seen other sicknesses come and go. I was just unlucky that I was the first one who got sick when it killed my mother and the others. I've learned not to blame myself, even if everyone else does."

She didn't sound as confident as her words.

"Yes," Breit said. "It's mean for everyone to blame you."

"I've seen you going up the stream a lot," she said. "What are you doing up there?"

"I like it. It's interesting to explore. I…."

"What?"

"Nothing," he shrugged. "You'd just think I was dumb."

"I'll think you're dumb if you don't tell me."

"I don't know how to say it. It's a feeling, not a thought."

"Try," she urged.

"When we went into the pool that time and got in trouble, the council scolded us for disturbing the pool. They said it is the source of our life."

"That's true."

"But it isn't. The pool isn't just here by magic. It comes from somewhere. From the stream."

"Yes," she nodded. "I see. You want to explore the stream, which is where the pool comes from."

"At first," he said. "But then it was more."

"What more could there be?"

"The source of the stream."

They were silent for a long time.

"Did you ever find it?" she asked at last.

"No. I went as far as I could, and the world got steeper and steeper, but there was still the stream. Sometimes it fell down cascades, sometimes it made pools, and finally it fell from a great height. But that was as far as I could go."

"You never thought of going farther?"

"It's very steep and high. Besides, what's the point? I'll be a man, soon. I'll have to go to work in the fields, and there'll be no time to explore."

"Yes," she said. "You'll be a man, soon." She sounded sad. "I hear you and Nesta like each other."

"Maybe if you didn't live so far apart from the rest of the people, you would know more about things." He said it a bit sharply, and instantly regretted it.

"I'm sorry," she said, tone turned cold. She got up to leave.

"Wait." Breit got up, too. "I didn't mean anything. It's just.... Look, Nesta says she likes me, but she doesn't even know me. It's not real."

"You don't like her?"

"Not that way. I mean, she's pretty and all, but...." Breit shrugged. "She so contented with life in the village. I don't think she'd really like me all that much if she got to know me better."

"Why?"

How could Breit answer? How could he tell her his blood was the blood of Arpad, even if her blood was tainted, too.

But, no. It wasn't. Not really. She'd gotten sick, and it was just that people said her blood was bad. But there truly was something wrong with Breit's blood.

"I can't talk about it," Breit said, turning his face to the pool and staring over its dark surface.

They stood like that for several minutes, like two deer on the brink of flight. At last, Riska moved, but it was not away. Instead, she stepped close enough to Breit that he could feel her breath.

"Maybe you can't talk about it," she said softly, "but I understand."

And then she was gone, leaving Breit alone at the edge of the pool.

The next day, Breit made up his mind to do whatever was necessary to find the source of the stream. If he had to travel for many days, he would do it. He would prepare while he had time during the long winter months ahead. In the evenings, after his grandfather had gone to bed, he went out into the shed and, beneath the cold clouds of his breath, began weaving a rope from the strong fibers of the reeds that grew along the stream just before it spilled into the pool. He probably would need it because of the steep cliffs that bounded the world.

During the increasingly frosty days, he walked as far upstream as he could, as often as he could, to strengthen his legs before the real attempt. As the winter progressed, the going became more dangerous because of the snow and ice on the rocky ground, which grew increasingly steep the farther he went.

But there was another reason for going that way. Riska.

After what she'd told him of her father, he was a little afraid that he might encounter him, and though he sometimes saw him in the distance, returning from the fields or a hunt, he never ran into him. But he thanked his lucky stars that he did see Riska. The first time, she was gathering water from the basin, and he just waved and went on by. But he was encouraged by her return gesture, and the next time, he stopped and spoke with her for a moment.

After that, the stops grew more frequent and longer. Sometimes she was at the basin, others she was tending the winter vegetables in the garden near the house or feeding the chickens. He wondered that she spent so much time on outdoor chores in the winter, then one day, as he was coming back late from a different direction than usual, he saw her standing beside her front door, staring through the dusk toward the path he usually took.

She's watching for me. The realization hit him with a thrill. She's waiting for me.

She turned to go back into the house, and he waved and called out. When she saw him, the worried look on her face broke into a smile.

"I went out early," he explained. "I was taking a shortcut so I could get back before dark."

"How far did you go?"

"As far as I could. There is a cliff, maybe fifteen men tall, and the stream falls down it. The rocks are covered with ice, so I'll have to wait until the spring melt comes to go farther."

"But then you will go up?"

"Yes." He didn't want to say it to her, but he had to. She knew by now that Arpad's blood flowed in his veins, though she didn't seem to care. But still, he could see a shadow flicker briefly in her eyes. He would go, and though they both pretended he would return after he found the source of the stream, they knew that something might prevent that. He worried that he would fall and injure himself too badly to go on or come back, and she worried that the stream would go on forever and forever and that Arpad's blood would heed its eternal call.

"Breit," she said, laying a hand on his arm. "I...." She looked down and laughed. Then she shrugged, put the hand around his neck, and kissed him on the cheek. "I think I see Father coming. You'd better go."

Flushing from her kiss, feeling something hot swelling inside him, he hurried off.

Riska wasn't the only one who noticed Breit's frequent sojourns upstream. That night, his grandfather came into the shed.

"Oh," Breit said, realizing that trying to hide the rope was futile. "I thought you were asleep."

"How can I sleep when your mother comes to me so troubled about you?" He pointed to the rope. "Let me see that."

Embarrassed, Breit handed the coil to him, and his grandfather examined it in the dim candlelight and tugged on it.

"It's a fine rope," he said, handing it back. "But it's very long to lead the cow with."

"It's not to lead the cow."

"Of course not. You wish to use it to climb out of the world."

"No, Grandfather," Breit said quickly. "Not out of the world. I just want to know where the stream comes from."

"Ah, the stream." The old man nodded. "You always loved the pool, didn't you? And the stream is what feeds it." He paused and stared deeply into Breit's eyes—so deeply the boy flinched but could not turn away.

"I can't help it, Grandfather. I.... I have Arpad's blood."

He turned away, then, ashamed of who he was, and worse, embarrassed to let his grandfather see his shame.

"The stream is a force of nature—part of the continuum of nature—and because it gives life to the village, it should not be tampered with," the old man said quietly.

"I would never do anything to harm the stream," Breit said. "I just want to see."

"I know you would never intentionally harm the stream," the old man said quietly. "But sometimes the seeing is what does the harm."

"I don't understand."

"Your father saw something, and it called to him so irresistibly that he never came back. That hurt the village, because we no longer had his hands during the planting and

154

harvesting. It hurt your mother, because it took her husband and the chance of having her second child. And it hurt you because it took your father."

"Did it hurt you, too, Grandfather?"

The old man was silent for a long moment, then he nodded. "Yes."

"Because you lost your son?"

"Partly."

"I won't leave the world, Grandfather. How could I? What else is there but the world?"

"Don't make a promise that you might not be able to keep," the old man cautioned. "The call of what you see may be too strong to resist, and promises will leave only guilt."

His grandfather rose, stepped across the shed, and took something off a peg on the wall. It was an iron hook that the old man used to hang up deer during slaughtering.

"Here," the old man said, handing him the hook. "Tie this to the end of your rope. You can swing it up to higher places, and it will catch so you can climb higher."

Breit took the hook, not knowing what to say.

"Thank you, Grandfather." He hung his head, then looked up at the old man. "I didn't think you'd understand."

The old man chuckled.

"I understand all too well. That's the other part of why Arpad's leaving hurt. Where do you think Arpad's blood came from?"

Breit blinked and felt his mind go blank for just a second. He'd never thought of it that way. And into the blankness flooded a whole new understanding. And a new question.

"Did you ever follow the stream, Grandfather?"

"I did. I climbed above the first cliff. I used this same hook."

"What's up there?" Breit was instantly curious.

"A long, steep meadow. Then another cliff."

"And above that?"

"I don't know. The second cliff was very tall, and I did not have the strength to climb it."

"Why didn't you ever tell me?"

"It's not the sort of thing a person talks about."

"I wouldn't have told anybody."

"It's not the telling, Breit, it's just not something that can be explained." The old man smiled and laid a gentle hand on the boy's shoulder. "It's the seeing. It's the experience."

"I don't understand. How can something happen that you can't talk about?"

"I hear that you've been visiting Riska."

"What?" Breit was as surprised by his grandfather's knowledge of that as by the abrupt change in subject. But then, his grandfather seemed to know everything. "Yes."

"Do you love her?"

There was only one answer to that.

"Yes."

"Tell me what your love feels like."

"That's easy," Breit said. "It's.... It's...."

What was it? It was warm and cold. It made him sing, but it made him feel intense. It was big inside him, but it was secret, too. How could he say what it was?

"You see," his grandfather said. "Some things can't be talked about, only experienced."

"But she knows how I feel."

"That's communication," the old man said. "Sometimes, when two people have a similar or linked experience, they can express their knowledge to each other. But it isn't talk. It's something that sometimes doesn't need words."

"Will we be able to communicate about the source of the stream when I get back?" Breit asked.

"I don't know," the old man said, rising. "We'll see if you come back."

Then he was gone, leaving Breit alone with the rope and hook. And his thoughts.

The next morning, Breit went down to the pool. It was very early, and the air was cold, but spring was near, and the pool was clear of ice. He sat on the bank and watched the reflection of the sun edge onto the surface from the far side and creep across, growing more blindingly brilliant by the minute. And as he watched, he realized something he'd never noticed before.

The pool was the same as it always had been. The stream came into it, constantly feeding it, but the pool never grew greater than it now was. He wondered at first that the pool always remained the same despite the steady influx, but then he thought about the many buckets of water that the villagers took out daily to supply the people and the livestock. And some of the water probably soaked into the ground. There was a balance between the amount of water that flowed in and the amount used by the village and the earth, and he saw as never before that the pool and the stream really were forces of nature that blessed the world.

Rather than deter him, the new understanding fired his curiosity and made him more determined than ever to follow the stream to its beginning. His rope was nearly ready, and he had the hook. All he needed was to gather some food and to wait until the elders proclaimed spring was upon them.

His mother sensed that something about him was different. Determined. She often was silent around him, and he would catch her looking at him with an unfathomable expression in her eyes. He knew he couldn't go without saying something to her, but he didn't know how to begin. Arpad had vanished, leaving her, and now her only son was about to do the same.

It was Grandfather who saved him. One evening, after they'd eaten their meal in silence and were sitting around the fire, his mother pricked her finger with her sewing needle, and though the tiny puncture oozed only a couple of drops of blood, she began to cry. Then suddenly she threw the shirt she'd been working on to the floor.

"What's the use?" she said in a voice filled with despair.

"Breit will always need warm, sturdy clothing from your hand," Grandfather said, looking up from the basket he was mending.

"Yes?" His mother looked up, eyes glistening with tears. "As Arpad needs them?"

"Breit is not Arpad."

"But he is leaving, just as Arpad left." Her voice conveyed the bitterness of an apple tasted before it was ripe.

"I'll come back, Mother," Breit said.

"You can't promise that," she said. "You only can promise to leave."

With that, she rose, went into her room, and shut the door.

After a time, Grandfather set aside the basket he was mending and went over to the shirt she'd left lying on the floor. He picked it up and laid it carefully on her chair.

"She'll finish it tomorrow," he said, looking at Breit.

"She doesn't understand," Breit said.

"I don't think any of us understand," the old man said. "Even those of us who have the same blood." He went back to his own chair, where he resumed mending the basket.

A few weeks later, the council announced that spring was approaching and named the day of the planting festival. As usual, everybody was there, though the food wasn't as plentiful or as fresh as it had been at the harvest festival. But everyone was in good spirits because the ground had thawed and planting would begin the next week.

While the children played games, the adults talked of the new season, making plans to ensure the best harvest ever. Breit spent some time with Slean and Earh, but both really were waiting for the dance to begin. Breit knew that Slean had been courting Nesta, and he told his friend that the two of them were a good match: strength and beauty.

"You're not mad?" Slean asked.

"No. Nesta wouldn't have been able to put up with me," Breit said with a laugh.

"You're right about that," Slean said, laughing in return and slapping Breit on the back. "But you'd better do something. There are only so many girls to go around, and most have their eyes on someone."

"I think Breit's been working on it," Earh said, glancing sideways at Breit.

"Yeah?" Slean asked. "Who's the lucky girl?"

"Riska," Breit said after a moment.

"Riska!" Slean laughed again, but this time there was an edge to it. "What do you want her for? She's sick."

"She's not sick," Breit said. "That's just what people say."

"Well, she brought sickness among us. Even her own mother died from it."

"Everybody gets sick," Breit said. "Everybody dies."

"Yeah, well, I just hope she stays away from me," Slean said. "You'd better watch yourself. Better yet, come with me when the dance starts. Nesta is friends with Estra and Anala, and they're both looking."

"Maybe," Breit said, more to get Slean to quit pestering him than because he planned to. "Right now, I've got to help Grandfather."

He didn't, really. He just wanted to get away. For the rest of the afternoon, he hovered around the edges of the celebration, looking for Riska. He saw her father, over with a group of men who were drinking wine, and it was obvious that he'd already had his share.

Breit didn't see Riska, so he continued to skirt the crowd, looking for her. After a time, bored, he stopped to watch the children play, when he felt someone come up behind him. It was Earh.

"I remember when we did that," Earh said.

"Yes."

"Soon it will be our children."

"I hear you've been seeing Mara."

"She likes me," Earh said with an amazed chuckle. "I didn't ever think any girl could like me like that."

"Will you marry her?"

"I hope so. What about you and Riska?"

Breit didn't know what to say.

"Riska is a good girl," Earh said. "She's pretty and smart. Better for you than Nesta or any of the others."

"A sick girl?"

"That's just talk," Earh said. "Like you told Slean, everybody gets sick sometime." He paused, then said, "I hope you and Riska get together if that's what you want."

"I think it is, but I don't know."

"You've been gone a lot," Earh said tentatively. "Exploring again?"

Breit nodded.

"Are you going to disappear like your father?"

"Maybe. But not because I want to."

"You have to find out something about him," Earh said. "And maybe about yourself."

Breit was surprised to hear such words from Earh. He was suddenly glad his friend hadn't drowned, though he hadn't thought about that for a long time.

"I won't disappear," he said, laying a hand on Earh's thin shoulder.

"Look," Earth said, pointing. "There she is."

Off to the side, Riska stood. There were people around her, but she seemed to be in her own world.

"I'll see you later," Breit said, leaving Earth and going over to her.

Some of the people nearby watched as he took her arm and went with her to the food tables. Breit's mother was there, helping serve food, and when her eyes lit on them, they opened a little in surprise, then a smile touched her lips.

"Hello, Riska," she said, handing her a plate. "I haven't seen you in a long time. My how you've grown."

"Hello, Nelda," Riska said, dropping her eyes.

"You should go dance after you eat," Breit's mother said, giving Breit a plate, too. "Young people should dance."

There was sincerity in her voice, but a touch of sadness, too.

"Maybe," Breit said, though he wasn't sure he knew how to dance.

"Come by our cottage sometime," Breit's mother told Riska. "You stay by yourself too much. It'll do me good, too."

"Thank you," Riska said. "I will."

As Breit walked with her to the trestle tables to eat, she said, "I thought she wouldn't like me." Then she chuckled.

"What?" Breit asked.

"Maybe she thinks I can keep you here."

Breit didn't know what to say, so he didn't say anything.

After they'd eaten, he asked her if she wanted to dance.

"I never danced," she said with a rueful smile.

"Me, either," he admitted. "I don't think I know how."

"Let's go for a walk," she suggested. "We both know how to do that."

They walked through the village as the air around them grew heavy with dusk. Somehow, they found themselves outside of the village, walking up the path that bordered the stream. Soon, they were at the basin near her house, and they sat beside it and watched the dark water trickle in and out, heading downstream to the pool in the village. They were quiet for a long time.

"Do you wish to lay with me?" she asked shyly.

"Yes," Breit said after a moment.

"We can go to my house. Father will be drinking all night and won't be home until after midnight."

"No."

"Where, then? We can go to your house."

Breit shook his head.

"I can't lay with you. What if I get you with child and don't come back?" He couldn't leave her alone with a child of his blood who might do to her as he was doing to his own mother.

"Then you love me?"

"Yes."

"I love you, too."

"When I get back, we will marry," he promised.

"Yes," she said, looking into his eyes.

He searched in hers for some glimmer of fear, but saw none. She believed in him, believed he would come back to her.

Would he?

"I'd better go," he said. "I have to get my things ready."

"You will leave early?"

"At first light."

She kissed him then stepped back.

"Go."

The next morning, he rose before the sky began to lighten, dressed, slipped out of the house, and went to the shed, where he'd stored his rope and meager supplies. He gathered them up in the dark silence then went out and shut the door. When he turned, his mother and grandfather standing there, their breath wreathing them in the chilly air.

"You would go without kissing your mother goodbye?" she asked.

"I didn't want to wake you."

"I wasn't asleep."

"Oh," was all he could say, and he kissed and embraced her.

"Here," she said, pulling away and handing him something. It was a coat, lined with fleece and fitted with a hood. "You will need something to keep you warm at night."

Breit took the coat, wondering when she'd made it, since this was the first time he'd seen it. He set his pack on the ground, shrugged out of his old and already too-small jacket, and slipped on the coat. It fit well and quickly made him warm.

"You'll need these," his grandfather said, handing him a pair of gloves. "The higher you go, the colder it will get. You have your rope and hook?"

"Yes."

"Then fare well, my boy."

"I'll come back," he said, but neither of them acknowledged the promise. Perhaps they couldn't. "Goodbye," he said.

"I love you," his mother said.

"I love you, too, Mother."

And then he was gone, hurrying down the street toward the path that meandered upward along the stream. The flow was beginning to increase as it did every spring.

Dawn was just breaking as he passed the basin where Riska gathered her water. She was not there, and it made his heart heavy, but then he found her, a mile farther on. She stood beside the path, waiting.

"Don't stop," she said as he came close. He slowed but didn't stop, and her fingers brushed his cheek. "I have you in my heart," she said. "Take care."

Then she was gone down the path, and Breit was heading upward in the growing light.

For miles, the path was familiar from his many excursions up it. But as the terrain grew steeper and rockier, he remembered only the more prominent features: this large boulder here or that ancient tree there. At last, he came to the cliff that had halted him in the past. The stream tumbled down its face in a merry cascade that made the rocks slippery and treacherous.

There was a way to the right that would take him part way up, but he'd seen that it ended in a beetling brow of rock that was impossible to scale. To the left, there was a jumble of boulders. This must have been the way Grandfather had gone, and it was the way Breit now went. The fall of boulders seemed to go on and on, but eventually he reached the top and found himself facing a sheer wall about twenty feet high. All he could see above were half a dozen trees overhanging the wall.

By now, the air had warmed enough that he didn't need his coat, and he took it off and tied it to his bag. The stream, falling some ten feet from where he perched, was out of reach, so he took out his water skin and drank.

After he rested, he uncoiled the rope and hefted the hook, looking upward. If he could throw the hook up there and catch onto one of the trees, he could pull himself up the wall. He tried throwing the hook overhanded, but the weight of the rope kept it from going high enough. Then he had an idea, brought forth by his memory of the way his grandfather had swung the hook back and forth on its rope before tossing it over a branch. So, instead of trying to throw the hook, he swung it back and forth on the rope and tossed it upward. The hook went high enough, but his aim was off. After a few more tosses, the hook caught on a tree. He tugged on the rope, and it seemed firm enough to support his weight.

He tied his bag and coat to the end of the rope then gripped the rope and went up it. In a couple of minutes, he was sitting next to the tree, dragging up his bag and coat. Only then did he turn and look upward.

As Grandfather had said, before him was a steep slope sparsely covered with trees, and between the trees bristled short, stiff, brown grass. Steep, ragged cliffs shouldered the slope on either side. He cautiously approached the stream, which tumbled down the slope before dropping off the edge of the wall he'd just climbed. Lying down, he scooped some water into his mouth, then he stood and started up the slope. There was no path here, though the sere grass crunched under his feet as he walked, leaving a trail behind him.

The slope went up for two or three miles, growing progressively steeper and narrower until Breit had to use his hands to help him climb it. Long before he reached its vertex, he saw the second cliff ahead, and it made his heart sink. This was no wall that he could toss a rope up to hook a tree at the top. There were no trees above, only rock that seemed to go up forever. The trees on the slope were the last of the forest, and as he sat, panting, leaning back against the base of the cliff, he could see the world as he'd never seen it.

The view was incredible. The world was, indeed, like a huge, irregularly shaped bowl, and rugged cliffs stretched out and rounded away on both sides of him into dim distances that finally were nearly lost in haze. He peered downward, hoping to catch sight of the village, but it was either too far away or hidden beyond the edge of the slope he'd just ascended. Two hawks floated in the air above the world. The distance was so great and the scene so wide that they seemed barely to move but were like leaves suspended in the still water of the pool, gradually circling.

At his side, though, was something that made him wonder about that still water. It was another pool, somewhere between the pool and the basin in size, but it's water was not calm and still like that in the pool or basin. It splattered and jostled and heaved as the stream plunged down the sheer face of the cliff and hit the surface with a thick, rushing splash. He sat in wonder, staring, not quite believing that the calm pool and pleasant, meandering stream that he'd always known could come from such turmoil.

He stared upward again, but the cliff must have curved back as it lifted into the sky, and he could not see the top or the origin of the stream.

He would have to climb the cliff.

But that would have to wait until morning, for the sun already was sinking toward the edge of the world on the opposite side of the vast basin. Breit didn't think he would be able to rest with that tumult ringing in the air all night, so he found a somewhat flat spot to sleep in a nook a hundred yards from the base of the waterfall.

He made himself a fire and fixed a simple meal that he ate hungrily. Then he took out the blanket he'd brought and wrapped himself in it, thankful for the warm coat his mother had given him. He sat there for some time, watching darkness filled the bowl of the world as the sun sank behind the far horizon. The edge over there, silhouetted against the red sky, was ragged in some places, smooth in others. It was, he realized, the rim of rock at the top of the cliff. The same cliff beneath which he now rested. Up there was the top of the world.

Then the sun was gone and the world lay in darkness, though the sky remained lit with a diminishing glow. Down there, somewhere, the lights in the village had come on. Fires and lanterns and candles would brighten windows with gentle, welcoming warmth. His people would be doing household chores, talking about the day, planning for the planting, and telling stories.

His mother and grandfather and Riska would be sitting silently, worrying about him.

The stars began to pop out, one by one, then in an increasing display that burnished the night more brightly than he remembered. Could there be more stars tonight than there were yesterday? Maybe Grandfather could tell him. He knew about the ways of the stars.

At last, Breit slept.

When he woke, the sun, peeping over the rim of the cliffs above him, had lit the far edge of the world, though the haze of distance erased details, leaving only a diffuse golden glow that faded as the sunlight crept down the cliffs there.

Breit performed his morning ablutions, ate, and returned to the waterfall. Looking up, he saw a rainbow arching downward, as if from the stream's hidden source. If source it was. He also saw that the cliff's face was not expressionless but was wrinkled and seamed, with many places where his hook might catch, allowing him to pull himself upward. Because the upper reaches of the cliff arced out of view, he didn't know if he could use this method to go all the way to the top, but there was little else to do but try.

So up he went, pulling himself from seam to wrinkle to seam. Occasionally, there was a ledge wide enough to rest on, but he couldn't rest for long. The cliff was very high, and after two hours, he still could not see the top. The higher he climbed, fewer and shallower were the wrinkles and seams, and the ledges were narrower, slowing his progress.

At midday, he no longer could see the ground at the base of the cliff, though he still could see the tree-covered slope up which he'd come the day before. From this height, the trees looked like tiny seedlings in a field. He was very tired, but he had to keep going because the sun would not stop, and he didn't want to be caught here after dark. None of the ledges were wide enough to sleep on. He climbed onward.

By the time the sun was just an hour from the top of the far edge of the world, Breit was so exhausted he didn't think he could throw his hook up one more time. But he did. He had to because the top of the cliff still had not revealed itself. And then a miracle happened. He came on place where a crack split into the cliff face a couple of feet, and on the lower end of the crack was a sharp little pinnacle of stone. It wasn't much, but it was enough, and he wedged himself into the crevice, then used his rope to tie himself to the pinnacle. His feet were dangling out over the empty space below, but for the first time since he'd begun his climb, he felt relatively secure. He barely had enough time to eat some dried meat and bread and drink a little water before darkness closed over his mind.

He awoke in darkness. At first, he didn't know where he was, only that he was stiff and cold and cramped and bound. He struggled for a moment with the rope before he remembered where he was, remembered that the rope was his lifeline and its binding his only security.

He could feel the cold rock at his back and the emptiness beneath his feet, then, but what arrested his attention was the sky. There were even more stars in it, if that were possible, than there'd been the night before. They sparkled here and shimmered there, and directly above spread a great, dense, dazzling sheet of them that was cut off by the dark mass of the cliff. The sight washed through him, amazement wiping away all questions. Then he slept again.

When he awoke, it was light, and he was immersed in impenetrable whiteness. At first he barely realized he was awake, then he wondered if he was dead. But various cramps and aches cutting through his numb exhaustion informed him that he was very much alive as well as awake.

Clouds, he realized. I'm in the clouds.

He found some dried meat and bread in his bag and ate, staring into the whiteness as feeling came back into his body. Only his body and the rock crevice into which he was jammed seemed real. The rock was wet, and that brought fear, for the wetness would make the rock slippery and the way above more treacherous than ever. And the thick mist masked any protrusions, ledges, and crannies above from his sight. How could he hook that which he could not see?

He would wait, he decided. Eventually, the clouds would move on or dissipate. An hour went by, or so he judged, though it could have been but minutes. It seemed like half a day. But however long it was, the whiteness surrounding him was no less dense than when he'd awakened. He drank some water and waited. The mists thinned enough that he could see the rock face diminishing fifteen or so feet away. He waited longer, but nothing else changed. The air was still.

He had to do something. He couldn't simply stay here, wedged in this crack until his food and water ran out. But what could he do? He couldn't see anything above.

Well, so what? He'd been climbing this cliff without seeing the top, merely supposing there *was* a top. Was this really any different?

Carefully, he unbound himself, then he tied the end of the rope to his belt so that if he dropped it, he wouldn't lose it. Wedging his left hand into the crack where he could get a grip with his fingers, he used his right to swing the hook back and forth, playing out about eight feet of rope. Finally, hope and confidence in his heart, he released the hook upward.

He heard it clang against the rock, then there was a skittering noise, and he pulled himself into the crack just as the hook fell by him to stop with a jerk at his belt. He pulled the hook up and tried again. And again and again. By now, his hope had turned to despair and his confidence gone cold.

But there was nothing he could do except try one more time. At last, when his arm was aching so much he thought it might fall off, the hook caught on something up there in the whiteness. He tugged on it, half expecting it to jerk free, but it held, and he pulled a little harder, then tested it with his weight.

He knew he was going to have to climb blindly into the whiteness. He didn't know what was up there and couldn't see how securely his hook was caught. He could be climbing up to a dead end, or the hook might come loose to send him plummeting all the way to the bottom of the cliff.

But there was no choice except climb the rope or remain wedged in this crevice until he died. Or go back. No! Falling would be preferable.

He untied the rope from his belt and tied his bag to it, then he started up. The wet rock made the climbing more difficult than it had been the day before, but finally he reached the ledge on which the hook had caught. Thankfully, it was wide enough to sit on as he pulled up his bag. He rested for a few minutes, then untied the bag, tied the rope to his belt, and swung the hook upward.

Eventually, it found purchase, and he went up again into the blind whiteness. And again up. After five climbs, the mists visibly thinned, and he could see the stream not ten feet away. And miraculously, he also could see the lip from which it spilled, which seemed to be the terminus of a rocky gorge, though he could see only the edges of the walls that rose on either side of the stream's sluice.

He threw his hook upward, into the sluice, and finally it caught on something, and he pulled himself up into the mouth of the sluice and lay there for a long time, completely exhausted.

When he'd caught his breath and his hammering heart quieted, he crawled over to the stream, which again was a merry rill instead of a shower falling fearlessly down the cliff. He dipped his hand into it and was shocked at how cold it was. Nearly as cold as ice. He drank, and the cold thrilled through him, clearing his head. He drank again, filled his water skin, then got to his feet and sat on one of the boulders that lay strewn on the floor of the gorge. To his left, the gorge wound up, took a further turn to the left, and was lost to view. To his right, the gorge opened into the field of whiteness from which he'd emerged. Above, a watery sun, well past midday, burned in a sky a deeper blue than Breit had ever known.

He ate a piece of meat then shouldered his bag and rope and started up the gorge. Many boulders, fallen from the bounding walls, lay in the bottom, whose contours were tortuous, with sharp inclines, twisted bends, and places he had to scramble to reach the next higher level. The air was very thin, and he gasped for breath and had to stop frequently to rest. Here and there grew clumps of sere grass, but nothing else seemed alive except himself and the stream. Always the stream, running through the bottom of the gorge, sluicing down a rapid run here, forming a shallow pool there, laughing as it went and cold as ice.

As he walked, the mists cleared from the sky, and gradually the gorge began to widen, grow shallower, and become less winding. And then, he came around a final bend and saw, half a mile farther on, that a wall of white blocked the end of the gorge. At first, he thought it was more rock, but as he approached, he realized it was a mass of ice.

And right in the middle, at the bottom of the now shallow gorge, was a dark hole like the Cave of the Dead back in the world he'd come from.

It was not a large cave, maybe eight feet high, but from it issued the stream. With fear in his heart, he went in. Unlike the Cave of the Dead, which was dark as night inside, this cave's walls held a dim bluish light as the sun filtered through the ice above. About ten feet in, Breit stopped, wondering if the cave was home to some wild animal, maybe a bear. But he didn't think so. It was too cold and wet inside, and besides, he'd seen no sign of animals at all since he'd begun climbing the cliff.

Suddenly a liquid chill hit him behind the ear and squirmed down his neck. It was a drop of water fallen from the ceiling. He looked up and saw more drops fall, each splashing onto the ice and rock at his feet to then ooze into the stream. He went deeper, and everywhere the drops fell and the cave shrank around him. And the stream was no longer a stream but a rill, then a rivulet, then a mere trickle. Finally, the ice cave was too small for him to go farther.

He looked back toward the entrance, and there were so many drops coming off the ceiling that it looked as if rain was falling. And from the trickle at his crouching feet, the running water grew along the cave's length to become the stream that flowed into the sunlight and plunged down the gorge and out of sight.

Breit wept, his tears tiny additions to the flow. They were not tears of sorrow, though he knew he should feel disappointment at the prosaic origins of what had been, until now, the greatest mystery of his life—that the pool so revered by the people of his village was simply melted ice. After all, he knew all about how melting snow turns into water and runs off in little rivulets. This was the same, just on a larger scale. He wept because he had set out on this arduous and frightening journey to discover the stream's source, and he had done what he'd promised himself he'd do.

But if the mystery of the stream was solved, he found himself moved with other questions as he hunched there in the dim blue light, feeling the weight of the ice above. There was still the ice above. The ice that made the water.

Slowly, he walked back to the entrance, where he stared up at the wall of ice. It was not a sheer wall, but more as if it was carved with huge steps where blocks of ice had broken free from the face. After the cliff, it was easy to climb, and he soon reached the top.

There, he saw a field of almost pure white snow climbing for another mile to reach the shoulders of the gorge, which also were shrouded in white. Up there was the top of the world, he thought. Up there is the answer to the mystery. He began walking upward, glad for his warm shoes, gloves, and coat.

The white beneath his feet was mostly ice, but in hollows here and there were patches of snow with crusty surfaces. If he stepped into one of these, his foot would crunch through and make walking difficult, but he soon learned to distinguish these patches from the ice around, which was rough enough that he didn't often slip.

And then the end of the world was just a few steps away. He stopped, suddenly fearful. What would be there, beyond the boundary? Blackness? Gray nothingness? Another wall impossibly high and impossible to climb?

But, no, the sky ahead was blue, and the sun always came from that direction. Taking hold of his courage, he went up the last few steps and finally stood on the very edge of the world.

He was high. Higher than anything else he could see. Over the top of the white ice field that was the stream's source, the ground fell away into another world far greater than the small one that had, until this moment, encompassed his life. It was so wide he could see no bounding wall on its far side.

Below him, the slope of white on whose crest he stood descended in another long field of ice and snow, and far below that was a lesser expanse of brown grass that, in turn, was replaced with a dotting of sparsely growing trees. The farther down this huge world went, the greener it grew, eventually stretching away into gray distances that were so far he could distinguish no features of any kind.

He thought of his fear that he'd never discover the source of the stream, and it felt puny now in the face of the emptiness that stretched in front of him. How far could this world go? Was there another great world in the dim distances beyond this one? How long would it take to reach it? How far did that one go?

By now, the sun was descending behind him, and he stood and watched as the shadow of the ridge on which he sat began to inch across this new world, just as it did in his own. With a shock, he realized that his own silhouette was part of the shadow, growing greater and greater as the sun descended and cast it over the land below. Somewhere down there, his shadow was touching some person he'd never seen and would never know. Was that person filled with joy? With sadness? With anger? Was he like Breit, or was she like Riska?

He shivered, partly from the cold, but partly from something else that he could not define. He pulled out his blanket and wrapped himself in it as the last of the sun went out of sight behind him, leaving both his world and this huge new one in mutual darkness.

He didn't know what he was going to do in the morning. The day had revealed such wonders to him, he had to think on them. Dream on them. Maybe in the morning he'd know what he wanted to do. Despite his exhaustion, though, he discovered he could not immediately sleep. The questions and wonder of the day would not leave him, and he pondered their meaning as the sky darkened and the stars emerged.

And as he looked at the stars, he recalled how his grandfather had likened them to the motes suspended in the pool, and he suddenly saw the spaces between them and himself

174

as one unimaginably huge pool. A pool so vast he would never be able to cross it. That maybe had no end.

Thinking of how important finding the source of the stream had been, he knew that the realization of the gulf between him and the stars should have depressed him. But somehow, it didn't. It seemed that, if there were only greater and greater worlds beyond his own, each filled with its own questions, then there must be worlds and worlds within the small one from which he'd climbed. And if that were so, then the questions and mysteries went as deep as they went far in the infinite distances above him.

"One pool," he murmured, knowing now that the pool in the village might not be anything more than water from melted ice, but it truly was, as his grandfather said, a force of nature, part of the oneness of nature. For the simple people of the village, it was the source of life, because without it, they would wither and die. But it also was connected by the stream to this other world, and that to the great pool of the sky above. And what lay beyond that? He could travel forever and ever and maybe never know.

That made him think of Arpad. Had his father gone on, down into this new world, seeking its secrets, seeking the next world beyond? Was he still out there somewhere, still traveling, neither—Breit smiled softly, now understanding—dead nor in the world?

At last, Breit slept, And dreamed. And in the morning, he began the long descent into the world of his birth. Riska would be waiting, there were crops to be planted, and there were stars to discover in the depths of his own heart.

RIMBEAU'S WOMEN

ART IS AN ILLUSION OF the senses, but one does not merely see the lifelike qualities of the painting or statue, nor do musical pieces please the ear alone. Words put together, whether denotatively or connotatively, are not merely descriptive. In truth, the illusions of art lie not in the deception of the senses, for the senses are fooled easily enough, as any parlor magician can demonstrate. It is the deception of those deeper receptive agents within the intellect and emotions that is more difficult to accomplish, whether the art work is naturalistic or not. Were this not the truth, all art that is not literal would be impossible as well as inexplicable.

But after all, we have the Surrealists, the Cubists, and the Abstract Expressionists, and the rise of these schools of art indicates that humans often have needs and goals that go beyond fundamental devotion to observable nature. We encounter particular emotional and intellectual responses to the stimulation of a given art work, whether the painting is photorealistic or fields of color, the music is a romantic interlude or atonal jazz, or the literature consists of expository writing or stream of consciousness. The sensations, ideas, and feelings engendered by a piece of art can be agreeable or not, but for a piece to be valid as art, they simply must relate significantly in all three spheres. This is the essence of art, not faithful reproduction. Faithful reproduction is just a style. The real question is how does the artist accomplish intellectual and emotional deception? I have an incident to relate that will suggest one possible answer.

It concerns Edward Rimbeau, the recently deceased artist, and took place twenty years ago. Since the subject concerns the nudes he became so famous for, you might say that the story does not apply to art that is not naturalistic, but I believe it can and does apply to all art. No doubt, Miro's shapes and colors meant no less to Miro than Rimbeau's nudes did to Rimbeau, though I'm sure in a different way.

Rimbeau had always been highly praised as a realist of the first order. His works brought not only a high price but critical acclaim. Then the women appeared, and afterward he painted nothing else. At any showing of Rimbeau's works, guests politely made the rounds of the landscapes, the seascapes, the cityscapes, and the other past escapes of Rimbeau's psyche, and everyone remarked how well Rimbeau painted, how lifelike, as if what you saw was not a plane of canvas but a window into the world. What everyone was really remarking, the men with lust and the women with envy, was just how well Rimbeau painted women, and each visitor managed to return to the women a second, a third, or even a fourth time to stare or gawk up at them. And why not? Women seem to bring out Rimbeau's genius more than landscapes or what have you. Rimbeau is not Gainsborough or Constable. Rimbeau paints women, so look, revel, enjoy his excellence!

I admit I'd done my own share of staring. I considered Rimbeau's women to be creatures of perfection, more real, passionate, and beautiful than any women I had ever seen. Life-sized and more true than the woman standing next to you, they seemed to stare out of the canvases, to look right into your eyes, to infuse your desires with some spark of their passions. Though they were nudes, there was nothing lewd or obscene about them, nothing to jolt the sensibilities or tease desire. Rather, there existed about them an aura of life and glorification of the body so subtle yet so strong that you forgot the people around you, forgot that the women were on canvas, in fact, nearly forgot that you were not and never could be as perfect or flourishing as they.

Rimbeau was in his early forties at the time of this particular show. He was of ordinary stature, and his features were a trifle sharp though in a rather pleasant and sensitive way. He was balding above the forehead, a fact that a rival painter joked was the result of long hours of hair tearing over incomplete canvases. Rimbeau countered that, in reality, he had plucked the hair from his head during late nights so he wouldn't have to wait until morning to obtain new brushes. Such a reply was typical of Rimbeau, who was neither the most brilliant nor the dullest of wits. Only his eyes were remarkable. They were a sort of blue-black, as if the pupils had enlarged and swallowed the irises, as if they were optical singularities somehow devouring the visual world.

Soon after I arrived at the gallery, I saw Rimbeau standing between a portrait of a city and a seascape's crashing wave. For some reason I had never fathomed, he did not like to be near his women during a show. He would supervise their hanging and then not see them until he came to take them down. It was almost as if he was embarrassed in their presence. They also had, I knew, the power to embarrass him out of their presence. Now, as I approached him, I could see they were about to do so again.

A young woman I recognized as being from an affluent family stepped up to him just as I arrived. She was very good looking, and I could guess what was going to happen. With small talk I did my best to help Rimbeau out of his predicament, and he tried very hard to skirt the subject of the women, but the young lady was persistent and finally had her way.

"You paint women beautifully, Mr. Rimbeau. So real and true to nature."

Rimbeau nodded his thanks, and the young lady went on.

"I wonder, could you use a model? I have some experience at sitting. I sat for Gregory Williams, you know. Maybe you've seen the picture? It's hanging in the Bellefontaine Collection."

"I've seen it," Rimbeau replied, and as he did, I remembered the painting. It was an excellent piece of craftsmanship, with the right amount of subtlety to raise it from being merely a well-executed picture of a pretty girl to an enchanting and provocative visual delight. It was not a Rimbeau, of course, but it was very nice.

"It is a wonderful painting," Rimbeau continued. "And you are very lovely, but I'm afraid I haven't a need for models right now."

"Yes, very lovely," the girl said wistfully. "But I'm not like your women, am I, Mr. Rimbeau?" She smiled at him. "I'm not...beautiful like they are."

"Beauty is in the eye of the beholder," Rimbeau quoted, fixing his gaze on the girl's face. "And, I think, it requires a certain maturity. In ten years, if you treat yourself the right way, you will have the beauty of the women I paint."

The girl blushed. Her eyes dropped then moved back to Rimbeau's face.

"Where do they come from? I mean, where do you find your models?" she asked.

"My friend here," Rimbeau put his hand on my arm, "has been, until this moment, the only person with whom I have shared this secret. Now I will share it with you, but you must promise never to tell anyone." What followed was the truth, and as far as I knew, I was the only person who knew it.

The girl nodded, so Rimbeau went on.

"There are no models. All my paintings come from my mind alone."

"But they're so lifelike. You must go by something...."

"Yes, but it is the convolutions of my psyche, not the contours of real flesh that guide me. The only reality my women have is as you see them. They are born on my palette, and they mature on the canvas. I watch them grow, and I give them life. Then I give them to the world."

"So beautiful, so perfect...."

"If they are, it is because they are my children, and I love them and want them to be beautiful and perfect. The only difference between you and them is that you are born real, with all the flaws and frailties of real flesh. My women are born an image, an ideal in my mind, and so are perfect before they become real."

Rimbeau stopped and turned his dark eyes to stare vacantly in the direction of his women. Then he faced the girl again.

"It may well be," he said, "that, in truth, you are the more perfect, for your perfection came after the idea of you. Your perfection is the labor of love; that of my women is simply the love of labor."

The girl averted her eyes for a moment before she said, "Perhaps I could watch you paint sometime."

A shadow of pain crossed his strange eyes. I don't think the girl saw it, but I did, then and once before when I had of him the same request. I anticipated his reply and the girl's sadness, and his reply when it came returned the sadness to me from where I had hidden it so long before. Who would not be saddened to be denied by a god the privilege of watching him create?

"I'm sorry," he said, "but it is too personal a matter."

"Yes...I...." She blushed, then, as she saw the pain, and she turned and gracefully fled.

Rimbeau faced me, and I looked into his strange eyes and could see in their darkness all of my own sorrow mirrored, magnified. I wished the subject had not risen again to plague me. I had believed all that hunger shelved far back in my mind.

"We are old friends," he implored me. "You would not hold this one thing against me?"

I wouldn't, I knew, but I felt that if I stayed right now, I might starve in the black holes of his eyes.

"No, but I, too, must go."

"Please try to understand...," he called softly after me as I fled from him, from the gallery; fled to some gaily lit and tinseled section of town. On this Saturday night, I hoped the sight of boisterous men and women might dispel all thought of Rimbeau's women. But the truth cannot be denied—what I desired of all things in the world, or above or below, was to touch one of Rimbeau's women. I want to take one of them—any one, which did not matter—into my arms, caress her, give her my love.

It did not matter that Rimbeau had said to me any number of times that he used no models or that I once had him watched to ascertain the truth of this statement. Not once during the course of several weeks did he take a woman to his rooms, nor did he see any, yet during that time, out of those same rooms came three of his women. I am not sure what I believed. Perhaps I thought he kept a woman in his apartment, though I'd been there often enough to know this was not the case. Yet I also knew that such reality, such life, could not come from nothing. I was convinced that he had to base his pictorial visions on something more than fantasy.

What I can see now but could not then was my own fantasy. I hoped that some of the power of Rimbeau's expression would be invested not only in the painting, but in the model herself. If I could possess, at least for a short time, one of his models, perhaps I could also possess, vicariously, Rimbeau's power. I was, however, blind to myself—or blinded under the spell of all the women Rimbeau had produced. He had created, amazingly, one of his life-sized women a week for the last three years. It was a phenomenal pace, but one he had, it seemed, worked into a fine science. He kept a strict schedule, beginning a canvas on Monday and finishing it on Saturday. On Sunday he relaxed and showed me his latest creation. I was always the first to see a finished work, but now, as I sat at a bar, surrounded by shallow and tawdry shadows of Rimbeau's women, I resolved that, this time, I would see the model he painted from.

I paid for my fifth drink, left the bar, and made my way to Rimbeau's address. I saw by my watch that I had more than an hour before the showing was over—an hour in which to explore for myself, at last, the truth of Rimbeau's assertion that he had no models. I ascended the stairs to his apartment, found the spare key I knew he kept hidden, and let myself in.

The lights in the apartment were on, and I thought, ah! the model is here! But she was not in any of the rooms. Finally, I came to the studio, my heart pounding, knowing she was in there, waiting for Rimbeau, thinking me Rimbeau come, waiting.... But the only item of significance in the studio was the easel, lightly draped with cloth. My chagrin at not finding Rimbeau's model vanished before the anticipation of seeing his next painting. I gently lifted the cloth covering.

I don't believe I have ever been so disappointed in my life as I was at the sight of that canvas. It was a lovely painting of a lovely, and yes, beautiful woman, executed in masterful brush strokes, with a tonal quality and texture that could only belong to smooth, soft skin covering real, firm flesh. It was as perfectly poised a painting as that which Williams had painted of the girl who approached Rimbeau earlier in the evening. It was definitely by Rimbeau—all the marks were there, as plain to the eye as the luster of her dark hair—but it wasn't really a Rimbeau. That special quality of truth, reality—call it what you will—just wasn't there, though the painting was photographically perfect.

Well, almost photographically perfect. Small sections here and there were not quite completed, including a portion of her foot and areas of her lustrous hair as well as the space where he signed his paintings. Could these small bits of imperfection explain the lack of life? No, I knew the explanation could not be contained in so simple a solution.

Rimbeau had lost his touch.

The moment the thought entered my mind, I tried to batter it down, tried to push from me the reality of that sudden, terrible conviction. I believe now my violent reaction was born out of the sense of loss I could not help but feel, for never again, I realized, would I ever see a Rimbeau woman in quite the same way. Never again could I even touch one with my eyes. Oh, there were all the ones he'd painted already, just as desirable and beautiful as always, but somehow their magic was dulled. It was as if Rimbeau himself were dead, and with his passing, all the true beauty of his paintings had passed also.

But that raised a sticky possibility. Could it be that art was art only because in it was invested some element of the artist's own vitality, something that went deeper than pictorial perfection or intellectual and emotional expression? Was there a sort of psychic bond between the artist and his work? But if that were the case, wouldn't the truth of any piece of art die with the artist? And I knew that wasn't so. Great works live on long after the artist's demise because of their intrinsic worth. No, that wasn't right, either. If it were, then the masterworks of the past would have as much meaning for a modern viewer as for a contemporary of the artist, and I knew that was not necessarily the case. My first thought must be correct: Art is invested with the artist's vitality, and if the work lives beyond the artist's lifetime, then it is due to the intensity of that vitality somehow preserved within the artwork. No, no, that was crazy, too, else the scrawlings of a madman would be as valid as sketches by Rembrandt.

I was confused. It was as if Rimbeau's loss of ability was my own loss of comprehension. One can define motifs, devices, cultural significance, or any number of terms to explain the impact of a work of art on an individual, but in the end, the impact itself cannot be defined. Then, as I was trying to define the impact that Rimbeau's lost touch had on me, the street door opened, and I heard Rimbeau's step on the stairs.

I must have been drunker than I thought for the time to have passed so quickly, but I was not too drunk to realize he must not find me here. He who had never let another look upon his work before it was complete must not suffer the anguish of being found lacking by some artistic voyeur. I recovered the painting and hid in the studio closet, thinking to sneak out as soon as he went to bed. Also, I'm sure, the desire to watch him work a little, even if he had lost his touch, was strong in me. Or, uglier, perhaps it was jealousy of something he once had but I would never have that made me stay to view in secret triumph his loss of that quality. So I hid in the closet, leaving the door open the slightest amount and positioning myself so I could comfortably see the easel.

His familiar figure entered the room and went straight to the easel and lifted the cloth. There he stood for several minutes, staring at the woman before him. I could not see his full face from where I was and so could not read his expression. But evidently his will had not abandoned him as had his touch, for, picking up a brush, he began painting.

He worked tinily, deftly, and with a great intensity, his hand jumping from palette to canvas, from one incomplete area of the painting to another and back to the palette. Now and then, he would pause and step back or squint sideways at the canvas, and each time, his return was more vigorous and, somehow, more aberrant, for the delicacy of his strokes belied the dynamic vigor with which his body moved. He seemed literally to dance in a sort of hypnotic rhythm before the easel. His exertions caused him to break into a sweat, and the moisture highlighted his cheekbones and glistened along his brow. Presently, he put his brush down and removed his shirt. As he did, I was startled by three things.

The first was the amount Rimbeau was sweating. I, in my closet, must have been much hotter than he, but where I was merely damp, Rimbeau's torso was drenched with a thick swelter. The second was the incredible change that the past hour had wrought on the canvas. I had been a fool to think Rimbeau had lost his touch. What I had seen before was merely the sketch, the foundation, the embryo from which life emerged. He had told the girl that his women matured on the canvas, and I had become witness to the truth of that statement. The canvas was now at least half as alive as any of the finished works I had seen. She seemed to poise there in front of Rimbeau as if she wanted to climb down off the easel. Third, I realized that Rimbeau must be mad; that I, in hiding and watching him work, had witnessed the insanity he had managed to conceal from the world, even from me.

As he turned and threw his shirt from him, I caught a glimpse of his full face, his eyes, and I was sure of my diagnosis. His features looked oddly discolored, at once flush and pale, and his eyes, those dark pools, were now glowing dimly, as if all the light they had devoured was luminating forth. I'd heard that the bodies of maniacs were capable of superhuman feats, and I shuddered least he discover me watching him. But I made no noise, and he turned back to his easel.

The ugly sweat now poured off him, and life streamed from his brush as he attacked the canvas in a near fury of devotion and concentration. Soon, he was radiating so much heat that I, in my closet, began to sweat heavily, too, and it stung my eyes and blurred my sight, but I was afraid to move, afraid to wipe it away, terrified of being discovered.

I blinked, and from his brush the strokes brought life, amazingly. The sweat was running from my hair and into my eyes now, and through the salty haze, I thought I saw his sweat mingle with the pigment, the pigment with his sweat, until he seemed to be painting with himself. He paused, plucked a single hair from his head, and, with his brush, stroked it into her tresses. Then he arched upward, kissed the beautiful lips, returned to his brush, and was it the light or the sweat of the heat and energy, or...her lips were so real! And as he delicately finished a toenail, caressing her arm all the while, why did the hair on my arm prickle? Where did his canvas end? When did I sleep and the illusion of thick, glossy hair cascading over Rimbeau's shoulder occur? Did he and she seem to fall together because it was I who fell?

Rimbeau's apartment was silent when I stumbled from the closet the next morning. He had gone to meet me for our accustomed Sunday morning breakfast. But the apartment was not empty. I could feel the presence of the painting, and I tried to look at it, but a sense of guilt and grief permitted me only an ashamed glance. That one brief look showed me the same yet now awful beauty that I had always seen but never understood, but it now divulged a terrible truth. With that realization came the certainty of my own contrite departure from the world where Rimbeau's women reign supreme.

I did not meet Rimbeau for breakfast. In fact, I never saw him again, though he tried often enough to get in touch with me during the years until his premature death. Nor have I again seen one of his women. I am certain the intensity with which I felt that final painting was not due to that particular painting but was simply invested in them all, where a discerning eye could easily see. Rimbeau's women, it is true, are visions of loveliness, but I think of Rimbeau's words to the pretty young girl, and I wonder if the rewards were worth their price.

THE NEXT STEP

"ONE HUNDRED THIRTY, ONE HUNDRED twenty-nine, one hundred twenty-eight...."

The numbers ticked off in Eric Littlejohn's head as he ascended from the subway platform to street level.

"...one hundred five, one hundred four, one hundred three."

He stepped onto the sidewalk paving and walked to the end of the block. When the red light changed to green, he crossed the street, counting, "One hundred two," as he stepped off the curb, and "One hundred one," as he stepped up at the other side. A few dozen paces farther on, he paused in front of a glass storefront, ignoring the hustle of the homebound work crowd, to look at his reflection.

The angle of light was wrong, and he couldn't see his slender features clearly, so he admired the crisp cut of his suit and coat instead. The clothes weren't expensive, but they so perfectly fitted his un-excessive tastes that he felt he couldn't have done better if he'd spent thrice the amount. Hanging his umbrella in the crook of his elbow, he reached up, adjusted the dim blob of his tie knot and the angle of the hat then tugged at the lower corners of his jacket to straighten any wrinkles. Turning from the glass, he reentered the stream of pedestrians.

Like most of the rest of these people, Eric Littlejohn was on his way home from work. For fourteen years, he had been director of the records department for a small life in-surance firm based here in the city. The work suited him, though it had been particularly hectic during the past year. Because he liked and identified with his work, he was as ef-ficient and courteous on the job as he was in his personal life. He didn't rush as did the hurrying throng around him. His was a sedate stroll, and he swung the rolled umbrella he carried no matter what the weather—you never knew when it might rain—like a walking stick, accenting his every other step with a brisk tap of the point on the pavement.

He sighed at the flow of people, wondering why they hur-ried so, then shrugged. Eric was open-minded enough to allow others their own quirks of nature. He just wished that so many didn't have the curious need to rush. But he was only three and a half blocks from the apartment building where he lived, and he felt that, even if he was one of those people inclined to hur-ry, he wouldn't do so this close to home.

He crossed the street, counting "One hundred," as he stepped down and "Ninety-nine," as he stepped up on the other side. Traversing the two remaining streets, he ap-proached his building, and started up the front stoop.

"Ninety-four, ninety-three, ninety-two." At the top was that odd step across the threshold, "Eighty-six." Entering the lobby of the building, he noted that Hamilton was in the sitting room, watching television. Eric resolved to call the old fellow for an after-dinner brandy and idle chatter on world affairs. Ignoring the elevator, he went to the stairwell.

"Eighty-five," he thought as he took the first step. "Eighty-four, eighty-three, eighty-two." He finally finished the countdown, "Four, three, two, one," as he firmly planted his right foot on the fifth-floor landing, then he pulled open the fire door and entered the hall. Within a minute, he'd closed his apartment door behind him and hung his umbrel-la, hat, and coat on the rack just inside.

The cozy, quiet apartment was a welcome change from the busy streets. Eric spent the next two hours relaxing, bathing, and preparing his evening meal. When he'd eaten, he picked up the phone and dialed Hamilton's number. After five rings he replaced the receiver, slipped off his house shoes, put on his street shoes, and left the apartment, locking the door behind. He went to the stairwell and started down.

"One, two, three." At last he reached the bottom, "Eighty-five," and walked across the lobby to the sitting room. Sure enough, Hamilton was still there, eyes glued to the television. Eric smiled to himself. The old fellow probably hadn't even eaten dinner.

"Well, hello, Eric," Hamilton said as Eric sat in the chair next to him. "How's life?"

"I take it one step at a time, Hamilton," Eric smiled, noting with satisfaction the return grin on Hamilton's face. "Anything interesting on the news?"

"Nothing new. More trouble in the Middle East, higher crime, more inflation, more taxes. Tell me something, Eric. Why does it always seem that more usually means less?"

"Is that the way it seems?"

"More or less," Hamilton grinned again. Eric chuckled.

He'd arrived too late to see the featured news items, and the sports didn't interest him, though because he walked part of the way to work, the weather caught his attention. After the closing up-beat news item, he asked Hamilton to join him for a glass of brandy. Hamilton nodded, pushed his aging form out of his chair, and followed Eric through the lobby.

"See you on the fifth," Hamilton said as he entered the elevator. Eric smiled and headed for the stairwell.

"Eighty-five, eighty-four, eighty-three," he counted as he ascended. "Three, two, one." He pushed through the doors to the fifth floor and went to his apartment where Hamilton was waiting. After unlocking the door, he ushered Hamilton inside.

"Go on in, Hamilton, and pour a couple of snifters. I'll join you in a moment." Hamilton nodded and entered the living room while Eric went to the bedroom to change into his house shoes. When he returned, Hamilton had set a snifter by his favorite chair and settled into the one across from it. Eric sat down, picked up the glass, and raised it in Hamilton's direction.

"To your health."

"To what's left of it," Hamilton grinned. "And to yours, my friend." They both took sips then sat in silence for a few moments, letting the glow of the brandy warm them.

Neither felt any immediate need to speak, for this was an old ritual. The two shared more than an apartment building, brandy, and the news. Though Hamilton was his senior by thirty years, this was the closest friendship Eric had found since leaving the confines of his family home twenty-five years before. They could spend hours discussing politics, religion, or society, and even if they often differed in their opinions, the disagreements were never more than good natured and stimulating. And, for Eric, there were other factors to recommend Hamilton.

In the first place, though a bit slovenly, Hamilton never disregarded Eric's fastidiousness, especially when in Eric's apartment. The old man loved cookies, which was a vice Eric, not having a sweet tooth, couldn't understand, and he thought nothing of leaving crumbs all over the chair in his own living room. Never once, though, had he left anything behind in Eric's home. He'd even take his empty brandy glass to the kitchen before leaving.

Eric appreciated this as much as the fact that Hamilton accepted Eric's other compulsion, that of counting steps. The old man occasionally made comments about the habit but was never malicious or derisive. On the contrary, he seemed, if not to understand, then at least to intuit the importance Eric attached to the practice. For his part, Eric valued the implied endorsement of his private custom.

Hamilton first learned of Eric's habit nearly ten years earlier. At the time, the two were barely speaking acquaintances, merely nodding to one another when they met in the building. One evening, as Eric ascended to his floor after work, counting as he went up, he passed Hamilton, who was on his way down. Eric must have been preoccupied, for he was muttering aloud the numbers as he passed the older man.

"Pardon?" Hamilton had asked.

"What?" Eric was puzzled that the older man had spoken.

"I asked what you said."

"I didn't say anything," Eric replied, perplexed.

"Yes you did. I heard you. But you must have been talking to yourself."

"Yes, I suppose I was," Eric answered, realizing now what had happened. "I was just counting the steps. Sorry if you thought I was saying something to you."

"I don't mind conversation," Hamilton said. "Lord knows I get little enough of it these days. But why were you counting the steps? I'd think there were enough of them to walk on without counting them all."

"Oh, but I do. Count them all. I...." Eric quickly shut his mouth, realizing he was probably making a fool of himself in front of this almost total stranger.

"You mean you count every step you take?" The older man sounded incredulous.

"Not exactly," Eric clarified reluctantly. "Only stair steps. Or curbs. Any step that goes up or down. It helps regulate my life. But this must be very uninteresting, and I'm keeping you from something...."

"Not at all, and I didn't mean to pry. Perhaps we could discuss it later. I like to hear about curious hobbies and customs. My name is Hamilton Beech. I'm in 767. Call me anytime. I'm usually in the building."

"Thank you for your offer, Mr. Beech...."

"Hamilton."

"Hamilton," Eric nodded. "I'm Eric Littlejohn, 539. Perhaps I will call."

They'd parted, Eric not really intending to pursue the old man's offer. But Hamilton took the decision out of his hands when he knocked on Eric's door one evening less than a week later. Since then, their friendship had grown to its present comfortable condition. And it *was* comforting to have someone to talk to, Eric mused, swishing brandy around in his snifter and glancing over at Hamilton, who was leafing through a magazine from the end table.

With a snort, the old man waved the magazine in the air, pointed to an article, and began to berate the government's foreign policy. Eric let him rail for several minutes, but as usual, Hamilton was a little off track. Funny how he could be so perceptive yet so naive. Eric broke in with a counterpoint, and for an hour they picked their way through the political salmagundi, refreshing their snifters in the process.

The talk finally drifted to personal matters. Hamilton told Eric the latest doings of his family, and he was all smiles when he mentioned he'd heard his youngest granddaughter counting flights of steps as she went up them.

"You remember her, don't you? I told her I know someone who always counts the steps he takes. She's only seven, but she was properly impressed. Of course, I said it's more than a pastime with you. More like a religion."

"I suppose it is like my mantra," Eric agreed.

"I mentioned that you count upwards half the way, then back to zero on your return. She asked why, but I'm afraid I'm not certain myself."

"It's quite simple, really. By doing so, I always end where I begin."

"She asked if you'd always counted steps, and I told her no, you only began after you were grown. She wondered if you were afraid that all those missed steps will catch up with you one day."

They both chuckled at this.

"You can tell her I'm afraid of the steps I might miss in the future more than the ones I missed in the past. After all, I began climbing stairs for my health. It's excellent exercise, as you know."

"So you've told me," Hamilton replied, "and I'm sure of it. I don't climb stairs any more, and my health's shot to hell." He raised his glass and tossed off the last swish of brandy. "Ah, that shot helped, though." He pushed himself out of the chair and took his glass to the kitchen.

"I'm afraid it's time I went home," he said on returning. "These old bones need their proper amount of rest."

"It was a pleasure having you by." Eric ushered him to the door. "See you tomorrow, Hamilton."

The next morning, Eric rose at his accustomed hour and prepared for the new day. Exactly seventy minutes after waking, he stepped out of his apartment, locked the door, and walked to the stairwell. He pushed through the fire doors to the landing.

"One," he announced as he trod the first step. "Two, three, four, five." He exited the lower end of the stairwell with an intoned "Eighty-five," and left the building. He went down the nine steps of the stoop, across the four streets to the subway entrance, and down the three flights of fifteen steps to the platform, where he waited for the train in prim silence. After it had come and he'd ridden to the station nearest his office, he started to climb the two flights to street level.

"One hundred forty-eight, one hundred forty-nine, one hundred fifty." He kept a straight face and ticked the numbers off in his mind. Reaching the sidewalk on two hundred nineteen, he went across the three streets to the building housing the insurance company, up the three steps to the entrance, and through the front doors. Seeing that no one was within earshot when he reached his office floor, the eighth, he spoke the last number aloud with some satisfaction.

"Three hundred sixty-five."

"Good morning, Mr. Littlejohn," his secretary said as he entered her office. Her matronly coiffed head bobbed a greeting.

"Good morning, Mrs. James." He unloosened his coat buttons and strode to his office door. "What have we in store today?"

She raised her eyebrows and pursed her lips.

"Too much, Mr. Littlejohn. As usual."

"Of course, Mrs. James. The dying make us work all the harder, don't they? Just a moment. Let me put away my coat."

The morning went smoothly enough despite the workload. At noon, he left the office, went to street level, and over to the restaurant he frequented for lunch. The total number of steps, as always, was one hundred forty-six. On his way back, he counted down, and stepped onto the landing of his office floor with "One." Once back, he regretted having had coleslaw with his meal, for raw cabbage, tasty as it was, always gave him indigestion. In his desk there was but one antacid tablet, wrapped in cellophane. He popped it into his mouth and chewed, chalkiness coating the back of his tongue.

Discretely suppressing a belch, though Mrs. James was still out to lunch and no one else was in the office, he eyed the shred of paper that had held the antacid tablet. He belched again. Realizing he was going to need another, he sighed, left the office, and went to the stairwell.

One hundred thirty-six steps brought him to the lobby, where there was a newsstand and candy counter. Exchanging pleasantries with the woman who ran it, he asked for the tablets, but had to settle for a brand in a foil roll. He then returned to his office, subtracting from one hundred thirty-six until he reached his floor.

As he opened the door, he nearly bumped into Miss Stevens from the sixth. She'd obviously been about to enter the stairwell. Miss Stevens was an appealing single brunette in her mid thirties.

"Hello, Mr. Littlejohn," she said pleasantly, pausing in the doorway.

"Oh, hello, Miss Stevens," Eric replied, feeling awkward. Miss Stevens always made Eric feel awkward when he encountered her, though he always felt a distinct gladness, too, and the dichotomy often confused him.

"Have you been to the Party on the Plaza, yet?"

"The what?"

"Party on the Plaza," she repeated. "You know, every Friday down at City Park. It's hosted by some radio station. There's live music and beer and pizza. Sort of like a fun happy hour. A bunch of us are going after work, and you're welcome to join us."

Eric didn't know what to say. He couldn't think straight. He eyed the doorway, wishing he could just disappear through it and bypass this entire conversation, but Miss Stevens was still in it, and there didn't seem to be enough space between the door frame and her breasts to slip by unobtrusively.

"Perhaps I shall," he managed to get out, though he had no real intention of actually showing up. But he had to say something to finish the conversation quickly and escape before his awkwardness turned into verbal clumsiness.

"Good," she said. "We're meeting in the park at 5:30. See you there."

At last she moved, though, in the confines of the landing, her arm brushed his as she stepped toward the up stairs. The contact brought a fresh fluster of confusion, but she was already past and, thankfully, didn't notice. Eric hurried through the door and, as it shut behind him, stood in the hall until the pounding of his heart slowed and his hands stopped shaking.

He really wished he wasn't forced into such situations. It upset his entire equilibrium.

He took a deep breath and headed for his office. On entering, however, the breath emerged as a subdued groan when he saw the loud suit and humorless smile of Jack Coleporter. Coleporter was the most obnoxious salesman that Eric had to deal with on a regular basis. Mrs. James, who was now back at her desk, raised her eyebrows and pursed her lips from behind Coleporter as the man turned to Eric and stuck out a hand. Resigning himself to his fate, Eric limply took the extended hand and shook it, trying not to inhale fumes from the man's liquid lunch.

"Hi, Eric, old buddy," Coleporter breathed in his face. "I've got a new data compression program you're gonna love." The salesman dug in his brief case, following into Eric's office. "I know your system's got some age, but this baby should work on your present hardware, so you won't have to trade in on something new. Can't beat that, can 'ya? Say, didja hear the one about...?" Eric sighed. Coleporter's tastelessness in suits was only exceeded by his tastelessness in jokes. With Coleporter droning on, Eric went to his desk and ate another antacid tablet. It was going to be another one of those afternoons.

Shortly after he'd gotten rid of Coleporter, Mrs. James came to the door. She'd received a call from the secretary to the company president. There was a management-level meeting in progress and a question had arisen concerning the parameters of the computerized filing system presently in use. Would Mr. Littlejohn please come up and give an impromptu talk? Now.

Eric got up, feeling a bit queasy. He hated giving impromptu talks, especially at management meetings. And not the least of the problem was that the meeting was on the fourteenth floor. Those were a lot of extra steps to take, especially considering he'd already had to walk down to the lobby for the antacid tablets.

As he ascended, he remembered Coleporter's comments about the company's computers. Eric was certain that management was considering switching over to a new system. The queasiness flared up again. He really didn't want to have to learn yet another system, though, to be truthful, the present system was ponderous, and he was swamped with a backlog of work. All he really needed was a little extra time.

Though the specific subject of switching to new hardware didn't rise at the management meeting, Eric was certain of a subtle undercurrent to the questions he was asked that pointed in that direction. As he trudged down the stairs an hour and a half later, worn out mentally and physically, he grimaced at the thought of having, once again, to master new computer software. Management probably thought it had the best interests of the company in mind, but didn't they realize the havoc they would cause in records? Why, it could take a year before Eric and his small staff got things back in order. Unless they hired....

He nearly stumbled on the next step as he suddenly saw his office inundated by a gaggle of computer brats just out of college, wearing nose rings and sweatshirts with holes and carrying sack lunches. The mere thought brought back the ill feeling in his stomach.

At last, he reached the haven of his office, and he plumped down in his chair. Looking at the clock and reflecting that the only good thing left about the day was the shortness of the remainder, he got back to work.

Finally it was over. Eric wearily plucked his hat, coat, and umbrella from the coat rack and left the office. With the numbers of the steps droning in his mind, he descended to the lobby. Emerging from the building, he had to walk around a gray delivery van discourteously parked across the pedestrian walkway. It was labeled with the name of some Greek firm, but Eric barely noticed. After the difficult day, he felt listless and introspective. Even counting the steps became languid and mechanical.

On the subway, he looked for a seat, only to discover he'd have to stand. He braced himself against a chromium-plated pole as the train jostled down the tracks, wishing the leaden feeling in his feet would stop. The latter half of the ride was lost in the oblivion of an imagined quiet evening at home with Schumann on the stereo and a glass of brandy in hand. Perhaps two glasses.

His brain numbered the steps as he climbed from the subway tunnel, but his mind was on his evening meal. Something simple and quick. He was mentally rummaging through his refrigerator as he ascended the stoop to his apartment building and crossed the lobby. Hamilton wasn't in the sitting room, he saw as he trudged to the stairwell. Just as well. He was feeling nauseous again and not at all in the mood for company. He entered the stairwell and began to climb, and as he did, the queasiness grew, and at the same time an uneasiness began gnawing at the back of his mind. It was as if, in his weariness, he'd forgotten something of great importance.

He turned from his mental view of the refrigerator, un-characteristically leaving the door open, and began to review the day's events. What had he missed? He considered each project he'd been engaged in, each appointment, every file that had been taken from its proper place. As he came to and passed each item he became more convinced he hadn't left anything out. That insufferable salesman followed so quickly by the management meeting must still be upsetting him. And all the extra steps he'd taken today hadn't helped.

Nevertheless, for some unfathomable reason, he felt extremely apprehensive as he neared his floor. What could be the matter? He shook his head, but the feeling persisted, and he couldn't understand or shake it. The feeling blossomed almost into fear as he turned the corner to the last landing before his floor. The leadenness in his feet increased until his legs seemed to be lifting twice their normal weight. What was it? Then, as he stepped onto the landing at his own floor and said, "Two," everything became clear.

He leaned against the wall next to the fire doors, breathing heavily, shoulders slumped. Sweat beaded his forehead. That was it, he realized. It was all quite simple, really. He'd missed a step somewhere. Miscounted. The day had gone badly, he was tired, and he'd miscounted. Gradually, his breathing subsided, and he smiled at himself. He hadn't realized how badly the day *had* gone until now. This was the first time in years he'd missed counting a step. Still smiling, he ruefully shook his head and pushed through the doors to the hall. A moment later, he let himself into his apartment and, soon after, was in a hot tub of water, soaking out the day's tensions.

Later, after eating, he relaxed over classical music and a glass of brandy, musing on where he'd missed the step. He remembered nothing unusual about his trip home, and after a few minutes, his thoughts progressed to the panic reaction he'd felt. Strange that his subconscious seemed to know before his conscious mind had that he'd missed a step, almost as if his entire biological pacing had been thrown off. It might be interesting to do some reading on habituation.

With a shock, Eric realized that he was almost thinking of his step counting as an addiction. His reaction was similar to accounts of addiction he'd read in newspapers and magazine articles. Though he hadn't known anything was wrong with his "fix," his subconscious had. He'd grown nervous and panicky and even sweated.

Then he laughed at himself for equating an innocent habit of counting steps with drug addiction. He realized that the physical manifestations he'd experienced probably were due more to the number of stairs he'd climbed today— something like twice the usual amount. Eric was well aware that he wasn't a young man, that physical activities were getting to be more of an exertion than before. Perhaps he should consider taking the elevator when he had to move around the insurance company building during the day. So thinking, he let himself drift into the Vivaldi piece he'd put on the stereo.

The next morning, as he prepared to leave for work, he resolved to pay closer attention and not miscount. Counting his way to the street and over to the subway station, he boarded the train with his usual aplomb, and was lucky enough to find an unoccupied seat. When the familiar jostling of the train halted at his stop, he left, added his way out of the subterranean passages, and over to his office building. He entered, a nervous quiver in his stomach, and started up the stairs. The quiver became a definite nausea by the time he reached his floor and put his foot on the landing.

"Three hundred sixty-four," he breathed.

One short.

He leaned against the landing wall, feeling faint. He thought he'd counted so accurately.

He rested there for several minutes, mind a churning blankness. Then he heard a stairwell door open two or three floors down and footsteps begin to trudge upward. Not wanting to be seen leaning here in this state, Eric hastily pushed into the hall. Mrs. James stared at him as he hurried across her office to his own, ignoring her usual greeting. Moments later, he was sitting weakly at his desk. She came to the door and asked if he felt ill.

"Just a little dizzy," he said, passing it off with a wave of his hand.

"Are you certain?" she asked doubtfully, lowering her eyebrows and pursing her lips.

"Quite certain, Mrs. James," he maintained, wishing she'd leave him alone. When she retreated from the door, he laid his head on the desk.

He was still there half an hour later when Miss Stevens knocked and came in. She'd brought a bundle of papers for refiling.

"Whatever's the matter, Mr. Littlejohn?" she asked solicitously, seeing his pallid complexion and tension lines pinching the corners of his eyes and mouth.

"Pardon?" He looked up blankly. Then his eyes focused on her. "Oh, Miss Stevens," he said. "What brings you here?"

"You asked that I return these personally to you, Mr. Littlejohn," she said, holding up the sheaf of papers. "Are you feeling all right?" She looked closely at him.

"Feeling...why certainly...I'm...." He looked down at his desk top. "I'm just a bit dizzy."

"Is there anything I can do for you?"

"No," he replied. "It will pass."

"Maybe you should go home for the day."

"Go home?" He looked at her, small astonishment in his eyes. "Why, I haven't missed a day's work in a dozen years."

He'd meant to express the pride he had in that fact, but the words came out querulously, snippishly. Miss Stevens' eyes flashed, and she dropped the papers onto his desk.

"Maybe it's time you did," she said, turned, and left the room.

Eric listened to the brisk swish of her hose as she went through Mrs. James's office and into the hall, wishing he'd reacted differently. Then he thought about what she'd said. Perhaps she was right. He was a terrible stickler for work. A day off would do him good. He could go someplace, a park or museum or such.

He stared at the papers Miss Stevens had left on his desk then fingered through them. He'd just deal with them first, then call Mr. Lasiter, his supervisor, and ask for the rest of the day off. But before he'd finished taking care of the papers, several other people entered in need of one thing or another, and before Eric knew it, noon had already come. Dispensing with his plans for a day off, he left his office to eat lunch.

As he neared the elevator doors, he considered using it to get to the first floor but passed by instead. He was used to walking down for lunch, and besides, he wanted to count the steps in the building. Perhaps he could find out where he'd miscounted on his two previous trips.

Reaching the lobby on the anticipated one hundred thirty-six, he felt a lot better and sauntered out the front doors. Exactly one hour later, he returned to his floor with a satisfying "One," on his lips. Entering his office in much better spirits, he spent the remainder of the day concentrating on his work and occasionally smiling tolerantly at his earlier behavior. The idea of taking a day off seemed ludicrous now. The afternoon aged quickly, and soon it was time to leave.

He gathered his hat, coat, and umbrella, left the office, and walked down to the lobby. One thirty-six. So far, so good, but half an hour later as he emerged from the subway station near his home, he found himself hurrying along the street. It wasn't that he'd missed a step, for he had counted quite carefully. Quite.

Unfortunately, he couldn't remember exactly what the numbers should be. He remembered the precise numbers within his office and apartment buildings since he often counted those as discrete sets, but those in between were vague and only partially recalled. That he simply had been living by rote through the years startled him, especially since he noticed it now only because the pattern had been broken. He crossed to his building, up the stoop, and through the lobby. As he passed by the elevator, the doors opened, and Hamilton emerged, bumping into Eric.

"Well!" Hamilton said amiably. "What's the hurry, Eric?" But Eric was already in the stairwell on his way up, leaving his friend staring after him.

"Pardon me, Hamilton," Eric's voice came before the stairwell doors cut off the scuff of his feet ascending.

Two hours later, Eric knocked at Hamilton's apartment. Hamilton opened the door, stared, then stepped back with a welcoming gesture.

"Come in, Eric. What's troubling you?"

Eric entered, as disheveled as Hamilton had ever seen him. He was still in his office attire, but the tie was loosened and askew, his hair a rumpled mess. Worse were the clenched jaw and the nervousness in his eyes.

"Some wine? Or brandy?"

Eric shook his head and stood there, seeming at loose ends. Hamilton ushered him into the living room and sat him down. Eric wrung his hands for a couple of minutes, staring at the carpet, then looked up at Hamilton.

"I've got a problem."

"So much I can already tell," Hamilton said gently.

"It's...it's got to do with step counting."

Hamilton was expectantly silent, so Eric felt forced to go on.

"I know it sounds foolish, but I've missed a step."

"Missed? What do you mean missed?"

"I don't know," Eric said with difficulty. "Somewhere between here and work a step is missing."

"Are you...well, of course you're sure." Hamilton looked puzzled. "How long's it been missing?"

"Two days."

"Which one is it?"

"That's the problem. I don't know which one it is."

"Surely it should be simple enough to find out. Tell me what happened."

Eric did. When he finished, Hamilton sat rubbing his chin for several moments.

"Well," he said at last. "Obviously a step has been removed somewhere along your route, most likely as the result of street repair, architectural renovation, or something similar." He got up and poured two brandies and handed one to Eric, who took the glass with a slightly shaking hand. "Maybe you should try to discover which one was removed."

"How?" Eric asked, feeling helpless. He took a too-large sip of liquor and nearly choked.

"I don't know," mused Hamilton. "Why don't you count each section of steps tomorrow instead of the whole lot of them? Do you remember how many were in each section?"

Eric sighed. "I can't remember the middle part." He took another, more careful sip of brandy, feeling better as the soothing liquid eased down his throat. "Maybe I should do that."

"While you're at it, look carefully for signs of recent construction." Hamilton smiled reassuringly. "I'm sure you'll find some simple explanation."

"Yes, of course I will." Eric took another sip, his hand steadier already. Gratitude was in his eyes as he looked up. "Thank you so much, Hamilton. I...I really appreciate being able to talk to you."

"Not at all," Hamilton replied with a warm smile. "Happy to help."

Later, in his apartment, Eric delved into his memory for the numbers of steps in each section of stairs on the way to work. The numbers for his apartment and office buildings were simple to remember for he often counted them separately. There also were a total of seven streets, which gave fourteen steps. He couldn't remember, though, exactly how many steps were in the stairs at either end of his subway ride. The only way to be sure would be to count them on his way to work in the morning. That night he had some difficulty falling asleep and spent the night fitfully.

He awoke groggy but determined to discover the answer to his problem. On the way to the office, he counted all the steps, but, instead of keeping a running tally in his head, he jotted each independent set of figures on a piece of paper. When he arrived at work he quickly added the numbers. His jaw dropped at the total—three hundred sixty-five.

He was still seated at his desk an hour later when Mr. Lasiter happened into the office and saw him there, hat and coat still on, umbrella leaning against the desk. Mr. Lasiter looked at Mrs. James, who lifted her eyebrows, pursed her lips, and shook her head slightly.

"How long has he been like this?" Lasiter whispered, stroking the dark line of his clipped mustache.

"This is the second day." Mrs. James was just as quiet.

"Mr. Littlejohn?" Lasiter said, entering Eric's office. "Eric?"

Eric lifted his head and saw Mr. Lasiter standing there on the other side of the desk. Strange that he hadn't seen the supervisor come in.

"Yes, Mr. Lasiter? Is there something I can do for you?"

"I was going to ask you the same question. Are you feeling well?"

"Why, yes," Eric lied and waved expansively to show he was feeling fine. "I...."

"You don't look well," Lasiter said, bending over and peering into Eric's eyes. "And look at you. You're still in your coat and hat."

"I can explain that, Mr. Lasiter," Eric said hastily, rising and making as if to remove his coat. Lasiter stopped him.

"No need," the man said. "I can tell you're involved in some personal problems. After all, I've been your supervisor for the last eight years, haven't I?" Eric nodded, and Lasiter continued. "I want you to take the day off. It's Friday, so that'll give you a long weekend. Take Monday, too, if you need to."

"But Mr. Lasiter, my work...."

"Your work can wait a couple of days. Mrs. James will fill in as best she can. You haven't been getting much done the last day or two, anyhow. Besides, you haven't had a day off since I've been here."

"I haven't had a day off in twelve years," Eric said, being careful with his tone.

"Then it's high time you did," Lasiter said. "I assure you that the office will manage without you for a couple of days."

"I suppose so," Eric said, moving hesitantly around the desk and reaching for his umbrella. Lasiter took him by the elbow and steered him toward the door.

"Now, don't you worry, Eric. We'll handle things around here. You just take care of your problem, and we'll see you next week."

"All right." Eric allowed himself to be led out of the office and down the hall. Lasiter took him to the stairwell and bid him goodbye. Eric pushed through the doors and started down the steps. He was slightly dazed by the events of the morning, and almost forgot to count down, but two decades of habit took over. Now that he knew there were

208

no missing steps, he felt he had to do something normal on this most abnormal of days by resuming his usual procedure of keeping a running countdown as he returned home.

He reached the lobby on two-twenty-nine, as he walked the distance to the subway station, he looked around himself with curiosity. He hadn't been out on the streets at this time of day in so long he'd forgotten that it would be different than what he was used to. For one thing, there were fewer people. He was usually out in work traffic or on weekends, when many people bustled about. Now, with the streets cleared of the bulk of the traffic, he noticed more of what was going on.

There was a woman pushing a baby in a stroller, a panhandler asking for spare change, two old women with lavender hair and fake fur coats, a messenger boy trundling a cart loaded with cartons. In fact, he was so engrossed in watching his fellow pedestrians that he barely saw the delivery van that almost ran over him as he stepped off the curb to cross the last street before the subway entrance. He jerked back just in time as the gray van zoomed by, whipping his coat tails around his legs. He stared after it, managing to catch part of the name lettered on the side as it sped around the corner. It belonged to an architectural antiques firm.

It happened so quickly that he didn't even have time to be frightened, though he felt his pulse quicken as he thought about possible consequences of not looking before crossing streets. Then, checking both ways, he crossed to the subway entrance. Boarding the next appropriate train, he took a seat in an amazingly empty car.

For the first time in years, he wondered what it would be like to ride to the end of the line. He had the time, and from the looks of it, he'd have the car practically to himself. But no, he shrugged. Since he was certain all the steps were there, he wanted to complete the counting all the way to his home landing. Reaching there on the right number would do much to resolve the conundrum of the past three days and restore his equanimity. Leaving the train at his home station, he climbed to street level, traveled the blocks to his apartment building, and went up the stoop

The sitting room was quiet and empty as he passed it. The stairwell door pushed open at his touch, and his feet took him up the steps. As he ascended, he began to feel nervous perspiration leak under his arms. The higher he went, the more he knew something was wrong.

"No," his mind pleaded as he approached the last flight before his landing. Resignation set in before he took the last step and counted, "Two."

Eric went to his apartment and dialed Hamilton's number to tell his friend what had happened. There was no answer. He almost cried but took hold of himself. The steps would have to be recounted, he realized. Right now. He left the apartment to retrace his route, counting each segment separately and arriving at his work floor with a list of numbers. Not entering the hall, he added the numbers while standing on the landing. After all, he didn't want Mr. Lasiter to catch him in the building when he had been told to go home. The numbers totaled three hundred sixty-five.

Eric nearly screamed aloud in frustration. Tearing the paper to shreds, he stalked back to the lobby, counting down. Half an hour later he emerged from the subway tunnel at his home end with the total on his lips, and stopped dead in his tracks. There, parked just on the other side of the street, was a gray delivery van with the name Thanatos Architectural Antiques lettered in an off-white on the side. He remembered seeing the van, or one like it, twice before. Hadn't Hamilton suggested that the missing step might have been removed due to an architectural renovation? It couldn't be coincidence.

A figure was in the driver's seat, obscured by the van's shadowed interior. As Eric started across the street toward the van, the machine's engine came to life, and the driver pulled off.

"Hey!" Eric called out and waved his rolled umbrella at the van. "Hey, there!" He ran the rest of the way across, but the machine drove away. Reaching the other side of the street, Eric tripped on the curb and fell, twisting his right wrist. He got up, ignoring his dropped umbrella, and ran after the van, calling for the driver to stop.

But the van didn't hesitate. In a moment, it turned at the end of the block, leaving Eric standing on the sidewalk. Just as it disappeared around the corner, a small white rectangle fluttered out of its window and settled to the pavement. Eric went over and picked it up. The rectangle was a business card headed Thanatos Architectural Antiques, followed by an address. No phone number was listed.

Eric stared at the card for several seconds, composing himself. He wasn't going to let this day get any worse than it already was. Pocketing the card, he went to retrieve his umbrella.

It was gone.

With slumping shoulders, he thought back to the number he'd been on when he'd emerged from the subway, subtracted the two street curbs, and continued on his way.

He reached his own floor on two, but he expected it. In his apartment, he took the phone directory from its shelf beneath the phone stand and thumbed to the Ts. He was going to call them up and give them a piece of his mind. It was bad enough they'd taken his step, but trying to run him down and taunting him were too much. He ran his finger down the list. Thanatos wasn't listed.

Eric pulled the card from his pocket and looked at it again. At least the place had an address. He abandoned the idea of a phone call, realizing personal delivery of his message would be more effective, and more personally satisfying, too. He used the phone to call a taxi then went down to the sitting room to wait for it. Walking down, he counted the steps, relieved to find they were all there. At least they hadn't taken the step out of his own home.

Fifteen minutes later the cab arrived, and Eric went out to it. He settled into the back, gave the driver the address, and watched the scenery pass. Within thirty minutes, the cab entered an industrial district and, shortly after, turned onto a decrepit street flanked by century-old warehouses. Ruts and deep potholes filled with greasy, muddy water caused the cab to jolt and sway on its suspension as it neared a mausoleum-like edifice fully a block square. Parked in front of the building, whose bare but grimy expanse of brick was broken near the top with a row of long, narrow windows, was the gray delivery van. The cab pulled up next to the van and stopped. Eric got out, handed the driver the fare plus a twenty and asked him to wait. Then he went up to the only door in sight.

The door's glass window was covered with a film of grime that nearly hid the tarnished gilt lettering spelling "Thanatos Architectural Antiques." Eric thumbed the old-fashioned catch, and the door opened, exhaling a breath of musty air. Inside was a square room lit by two dusty florescent tubes. A desk behind a wooden railing that looked like an old balustrade faced a fifteen foot wooden pew. No one was in the room. Eric sat stiffly on the pew, feeling conspicuous, and eyed the door in the wall behind the desk.

After several minutes, when no one came, Eric got up, went around the end of the railing to the door, and opened it. Beyond was a vast space echoing shadows. The part of it that Eric could see was dimly lit by intermittent single-globe fixtures hanging on long wires from a ceiling lost in darkness. Large, oddly shaped, shadowy heaps lay everywhere on the floor.

"Hello," he called out, and his voice was swallowed almost instantly by the emptiness. "Anyone there?"

This is foolish, he thought. I'll just leave. Thanatos can have the step. It doesn't matter. I'll just have to adjust.

He backed out of the warehouse, walked across the office, and went outside.

The cab was gone.

Damn, he thought, looking up and down the rutted street. The Thanatos van was the only vehicle in sight.

Realizing he'd have to go back inside, if for no other reason than to find a telephone to call another cab, he returned to the front office. The desk behind the balustrade was barren of anything save an old-fashioned banker's lamp, green shade strung with cobwebs. Maybe there's a phone in the warehouse, he thought. There must be a telephone.

Once again, he opened the door to the warehouse and entered the hugely shadowed space. Letting the office door swing shut behind him, he walked across the warehouse floor, looking for a sign of anyone. His feet carried him past the first dimly lit pile, and he noted that it contained numerous pieces of balustrades and banisters in many colors and designs. Next to that were several six-foot stacks of French doors, and beyond those was a thirty-foot row of fireplace mantles standing face to back. Eric had just bent to look through the tunnel-like space formed by their openings when he heard a clatter come from off to his right.

"Hello?" His voice seemed to be sucked into the darkness of the rafters. "Hello?"

No answer came, so Eric moved in the direction from which the sound emanated. Past a huge jumble of wrought iron fencing were eight formidable stacks of polished wooden doors and a large cupola with a sailing ship weather vane. There he came up against a wall. Dozens of decorative, leaded glass windows leaned against it, opaque with grime and dimness.

Eric walked down the wall and came to a forest of columns and pillars supporting nothing. He was reluctant to walk through such a precarious grove, but as his way around was blocked on one side by the wall and on the other by six or seven identical gables strung out into the darkness, he decided to go ahead.

Taking care not to brush against any of the columns least he topple the whole lot, Eric sidled through the truncated arbor. On the other side, he found himself confronted by hundreds upon hundreds of lawn statues of every conceivable subject and shape. He was somewhat taken aback when he squeezed through the last row of columns and saw them, for they all seemed to be looking right at him. Barely breathing, he gingerly picked his way among them. After fifty feet the lawn statues were replaced by gargoyles.

"There must be more here than at Notre Dame," Eric muttered. Suddenly his foot caught on a gape-mouthed demon, and he crashed to the floor. His head struck another gargoyle, and he lay stunned for several moments.

When at last he opened his eyes and focused his swimming vision, he saw a leering, wild-eyed stone face sticking its forked tongue at him. He groaned and shielded his eyes then felt his head where it had been hit. No blood was apparent, though a large knot welted under the hair. Rolling over, he got to all fours, wooziness washing through him.

He'd never be able to walk through this hellish assembly, so he even didn't try. Past gape, scowl, yawp, and goggle he crawled until, at last, knees sore and hands filthy, he emerged from the field of gargoyles. By this time, his head had cleared, and he stood up, bracing himself against the large corkscrew of one of two iron spiral staircases, white paint showing spots of rust, lying side by side. He felt the rising lump again, realizing he'd lost his hat in the fall. Then he let go of the spiral staircase and bent to brush himself off. Straightening, he gasped and took a step backwards.

There in front of him stood a man. He was stocky, slightly taller than Eric, with straight, block-cut dark hair that was graying at the temples, heavy features, and deep-set eyes. He was wearing dark trousers held by suspenders and a white shirt with the sleeves rolled to his elbows. He looked to be in his fifties, but he could have been older.

"I fell and hurt myself," Eric said, waving vaguely in the direction of the gargoyles.

"Yes. One must be careful among those little devils," the man said, giving a shallow smile that showed only the blunt tips of his front teeth. It was peculiar how only his upper lip moved to make the smile. "I hope you didn't break anything."

"No. I bumped my head, but I'm sure nothing is broken," Eric assured him then suddenly realized that the man might be referring to his merchandise.

"Hmm," came the noncommittal reply then a pause that was just long enough to set Eric on edge. "And what may I do for you, sir?"

"Is this your card?" Eric fished in his pocket, drew out the rectangle of paper, and handed it to the man. The fellow looked at it for a moment.

"Yes, it is," he said and pocketed it. "Thank you for returning it." The pause came again. "Was there something else?"

"Yes," Eric said hesitantly. "There was. A step...."

"You wish to purchase a step? Right this way." Before Eric could protest, the man turned on his heel and disappeared around the spiral staircases.

Eric followed. A short distance away the man halted beside a tremendous pile of steps and stoops of all sizes, shapes, and descriptions, piled and jumbled together like a bunch of building blocks that might belong to a huge child.

"Here is our selection," the man said as Eric came up to the pile. "If you see anything you like, just point it out."

"No," Eric said. "You don't understand. I'm not looking for any step. I want a particular one."

"Sir?" The man sounded curious, but he didn't look that way. His face seemed rather immobile.

"I mean...." Eric stopped, wondering what he *did* mean. What had he come here for, anyway? He couldn't tell this man the truth. When he shook his head to clear it, the knot on his scalp throbbed. The tension of the last three days finally was descending on him. His own inability to say what he wanted jarred against this man's impenetrable demeanor.

"I'm missing a step," he said, having difficulty keeping his voice level. "It was there three days ago, had been for years. Now it's gone. I want to find it."

The man put his hands behind his back and shifted his weight slightly. "What does this step look like, sir? If you could describe it, perhaps...."

"I don't know what it looks like!" Eric cried out. He grabbed at the man, but the other casually struck down his arm. Eric felt dizziness and shame spin in him, and he hung his head. "I don't know what it looks like," he repeated in a quieter tone. "I don't know which one it was. I saw your truck. I found your card...."

"Ah, yes," The man's eyes glittered in his motionless features. Then the upper lip raised again in that peculiar smile. "Follow me, sir. I do have one last step over here. Perhaps it is the one you seek."

Eric trailed after him through the dim space. In twenty paces, the dimness grew darker still, until Eric could no longer see the man, only hear him. He wished he had his umbrella to feel the way in front of him, but it was gone.

216

Then ahead he saw a flash of light. In its momentary glow, he saw the man moving deliberately through a forest of upright shapes. Then another flash illuminated the scene, but from a different angle. Then a third.

Eric realized he was following the man through a forest of wrought iron lamp poles, each with one or more decorative globes or glass flower petals encasing the lamps. The lamps were flashing one at a time, at odd intervals and in no particular order, bewildering Eric's vision and his sense of direction. After a few moments he lost sight of the man. He turned one way then another, eyes drawn by puddle after puddle of light, searching for the man, or at least some way out of this maddening glimmer. Within a minute, he was totally lost and confused. Sweat had taken the starch out of his shirt.

"Hello!" he called nervously.

"How long have you been seeking this step?" The man's voice was a harsh whisper in Eric's ear, and Eric nearly jumped out of his skin.

"Three days." Eric's voice was a panting quaver. "I told you, three days."

The man gave him that peculiar stare again as the flashing lights lit him from every conceivable angle. Then he gestured with his arm away to the left.

"This way, sir."

Eric followed the man out of the lamp pole forest and ahead saw a steady light in a glittering mass suspended a dozen feet above the floor. As he approached, Eric realized that the glittering mass was an ornate crystal chandelier lit by a single bulb. In the fractured pool of light cast onto the floor was a large, sheet-covered, rectangular shape. The man stopped by the object and waited for Eric to draw closer.

217

"I believe this might be what you are looking for, sir." He bent, grasped the corner of the sheet, and whipped it off the object.

Dust puffed into Eric's face, and he stepped back, coughing and batting at the air. For a terrible second, he thought that the rectangular object would be a coffin, then, through watering eyes, he saw that it was, indeed, a step, though it was the biggest one he'd ever seen. If the jumble of steps he'd seen earlier were like the toy blocks of a giant child, this was that child's step. Fully three feet high, wide, and deep and seven long, it was made of dark, heavy wood.

Eric peered at its polished surface then up at the man.

"No," he said, knees growing weak. "I don't think that's the step. It's much too big. I'd have remembered if...."

"Look closer, sir," the man insisted, taking Eric's elbow and drawing him nearer. "Are you certain? Feel the texture of the wood." He pulled Eric's hand onto the step. The texture was very smooth. "We use only the finest mahogany."

The man let go of his arm, and Eric's hand lingered on the smooth, cool surface for a moment before he retracted it.

"Let me show you this special feature."

The man guided Eric around to the end of the step and urged him right up to it until Eric's knees were touching the wood. Then he bent and, with a deftly dramatic movement, pulled up on the top of the step, which swung open, creaking, like a hinged lid.

Eric's jaw dropped in disbelief at the black pit yawning beneath the opening. Dimly illuminated by the bulb overhead was a long flight of grimy, damp-looking stone stairs leading down into the pitch. Giddiness nauseated him, and he passed a hand over his face. But the black pit was still there when he opened his eyes.

"...many steps in one," the man was saying. With a gasp, Eric tried to back up, but the man was standing inexplicably close, and he bumped right into him. Eric's knees buckled, and he fell forward into the opening. Chilly dampness breathed across his face, and he barely got his hands outstretched in front of himself to break his fall. His shins scraped painfully on the wood, then all of a sudden the light went out as the step's lid slammed shut on top of him.

Eric shouted, half in fear, half in pain, as the lid pinioned both of his legs partly outside the step. He put his hands flat on the top step, grimacing at the slimy feel of the tread, and strained against the weight of the lid.

Why couldn't he lift the lid? It was so heavy, though the man had lifted it easily enough. Still wrenched from his fall on the street, his right wrist twisted again, shooting pain through his forearm. The palm slipped off the mucilaginous surface and slapped against the next lower step.

"One." The number ticked off so automatically in his mind that he didn't really notice it. He had so much more to think about as he slid a little further down the stairs, painfully dragging his shins against the edge of the step.

Eric shouted again and pushed desperately upward, lashing out with his feet at the same time. The exertion only caused his hand to slip another step further down. More skin scraped from his shin.

"Two."

He heard the number, then, and the "three" that followed when his hand skidded to a still lower tread, leaving him almost fully extended down into the hole.

The numbers galvanized him with an awful fascination that took but a moment to erupt into complete terror. This time he did not shout. He screamed with unholy desperation.

Lashing out again with his feet, he didn't even notice that, as his hand slipped one step further down, he failed to count. He knew only that the heel of his shoe connected with something, and the intolerable weight of the lid abruptly eased.

He heaved the lid up, dragged himself out of the open step, and rolled to the floor. A few feet away, Thanatos was bent over, rubbing a knee. Eric scrambled to his feet as the man straightened and took a step toward him. Eric moaned, turned, and fled through the darkness.

"Don't you wish to take the step, sir?" the man called after him, but Eric paid no mind.

Somehow he found his way through the bewildering forest of flashing lights and the maze of antique junk littering the warehouse. After blinding, fearful minutes, he staggered into the office and a moment later burst outside, letting the door crash open. Hearing sounds from the dusky space beyond the confined office, he turned blindly to the rutted street and ran, his feet splashing into and out of the deep potholes and ruts. Down the street he ran on legs strengthened by years of stair climbing. With nary a number on his lips or in his mind, he ran and ran.

Not long after, Hamilton rode the elevator down to the lobby of the apartment building. As the doors opened and he emerged, he was amazed to see a hatless, disheveled Eric Littlejohn bound up the stoop, two steps at a time, rush across the lobby, and brush past him into the elevator. Before Hamilton could collect himself enough to say a word, Eric reached out and punched a button.

"Sorry, Hamilton," Eric called out. "I have to be at City Park by 5:30."

The doors slid shut, and the numbers on the floor indicator lit as the elevator ascended.